Shandra Higheagle Mystery Books

Double Duplicity

Tarnished Remains

Deadly Aim

Murderous Secrets

Killer Descent

Reservation Revenge

Yuletide Slaying

Fatal Fall

Haunting Corpse

Artful Murder

Shandra Higheagle Mystery

Paty Jager

Windtree Press

Hillsboro, Or

ARTFUL MURDER

Contact Information: info@windtreepress.com

Windtree Press
Hillsboro, Oregon
http://windtreepress.com

Cover Art by Christina Keerins

Published in the United States of America

ISBN 9781947983274

Acknowledgement

While I hope the incidents that happen in this book never happen to this magnitude in a school, it is a subject that can, and is, in some schools not addressed.

Chapter One

Shandra Higheagle walked into the Art Quad at Warner High School and discovered a student backing the scrawny, weaselly art teacher up against the wall.

"Mr. Huntley, I don't care if you are an adult or a teacher, you don't treat my brother like he doesn't have feelings. Because he does." Boyd Lange, the star basketball player and older brother to Travis, a student with Autism, looked as if he would like to pluck Mr. Huntley's poor excuse of a mustache out one whisker at a time.

"Boyd!" Shandra hurried forward as fast as she could with her wet soled cowboy boots slipping on the vinyl flooring.

The student glanced her way, shook the teacher, and

shoved him against the wall before running down the hall and out a back door.

"Mr. Huntley, are you hurt?" she asked, hoping her simple question didn't make him think she was interested in him. He was known among the female teachers as a pathetic man who took any sign of interest in him as an opening to think they were an item.

He shook himself like a dog and settled his open-necked shirt, which showed too much of his spindly-haired chest, back in place. "I'm fine. That boy is touchy when it comes to his brother."

"It's not touchy, it's protective." She peered down at the man, four inches shorter than herself. "I've heard you belittle Travis in front of the other students. Your disregard for his feelings leaves him open to the other students taunting him."

The teacher curled his lip in distaste. "Another do-gooder. That boy shouldn't be here. He belongs in a special school."

She shook her head. "No, he doesn't. He just has to process things differently than the rest of us. He's smarter and more talented than you." Shandra pivoted on her boot heel and headed to the room she'd occupied this third quarter of the school year as a volunteer pottery teacher.

The bell for her next class rang, and students began filing in. She smiled and greeted each by their name. As the last bell buzzed through the drone of voices, noting class was to begin,
Shandra scanned the room to make sure everyone was ready. Travis wasn't at his pottery wheel.

"Has anyone seen Travis?" she asked.

"He was sitting in the commons in a corner mumbling to himself," Sally offered.

"You can all start working on your projects. I'll be right back." Shandra grabbed her coat off her chair and headed out of the room. She left the building through the front entrance, following the sidewalk to the entrance of the main building and the common area where students ate lunch. Even though it was mid-March, there were still spots of snow and ice on the walkway between the two buildings.

The notion to hurry, hammered in her head. Why, she didn't know.

Inside the main building, she blinked to get her eyes accustomed to the indoor lighting versus the brightness of the piles of snow outside.

Mr. Pawner, the principal, hovered in the far corner of the commons. She headed across the room and spotted Travis hunched at a table.

The principal turned at the sound of her boot heels on the hard vinyl floor. "Ms. Higheagle, don't you have a class?"

"Yes. And Travis is missing it." She dropped to a crouch beside the distraught boy. "Travis? It's Ms. Higheagle."

He continued mumbling but flicked a gaze her direction.

"You're missing class. You like how the clay feels slipping through your fingers. Remember?" She made the motion of molding clay spinning on a wheel.

Travis turned his head, watching her hands.

"Don't you want to come finish the pot you're making for your mother?" Shandra held out her hand to the young man.

He nodded and put his hand in hers. She noticed he still had patches of paint from his class before lunch with Mr. Huntley. It was obvious the teacher had said something that made the boy run out of class without washing up. Whatever the man had said, Boyd had discovered.

She rose, drawing Travis to his feet. "Mr. Pawner, we're going to class."

Travis didn't look at the principal. His head was downcast, and his lips still moved as he mumbled, but he walked alongside Shandra through the commons, outside, and into the Art Quad.

When they entered the room, all talking stopped. She led Travis to his wheel and began her inspection of the other students' work. Out of the corner of her eye, she watched as the boy uncovered his work and began remolding the pot.

Nancy Tait, the special education teacher, arrived at the first buzz of the end of class bell.

Shandra walked over to the woman, waiting for Travis to cover his work. "Mr. Huntley said something to him in art class before lunch. You might want to talk to him about not taking what that man says to heart."

Nancy's brown pixie cut hair revealed her red tipped ears. It was apparent even though she didn't say anything, she was angry with the art teacher. "I'll do my best to let

Travis know not to allow that man to ruin his day." She walked over, put an arm around the boy's shoulders, and led him out of the room, talking softly.

Shandra cleaned up the room and gathered her belongings. She'd offered to volunteer in the art department at Warner High last fall on a whim. But she'd enjoyed working with the students every day this quarter. The best part was being able to work on her art in the mornings before coming in to the class before lunch, spending lunch visiting with the teachers, and then teaching the after-lunch period and going home.

She smiled. Well, home for the last six weeks. Ryan's house in Warner. They'd brought her traveling pottery wheel, buckets of clay, and Sheba to Warner the week before she'd started volunteering. They went to her house on the weekends, but she had to admit, living in town had its perks.

Like now. She'd ordered pizza to go from the best pizza restaurant this morning and would pick it up on her way home. Since Ryan hadn't texted he'd be late, they'd spend the evening watching movies and eating pizza.

Before she could leave, Shandra had to check into the

office and let Rachel, the secretary, know she was leaving for the day. She followed the sidewalk to the main entrance and stopped at the small window in front of the secretary's desk.

"Shandra, all done for the day?" Rachel ran one hand of flashy fingernails through her short, cherry red hair.

"I am. It's hard to believe there is only a week and a half left in this quarter and I'll be done." Last night when Ryan brought up the fact she would be moving back to her ranch on Huckleberry Mountain in two weeks, sadness had swamped her. She'd never thought of herself as a teacher, but then, she'd always enjoyed teaching workshops at art events.

"I'm sure your students have learned a lot from you. Maybe you could do this again next year." Rachel slid the sign-out board across the small counter.

Shandra signed. "That would be fun. I'll have to talk to Ms. Tierney and Mr. Pawner about it."

Gertrude Miller, the media center instructor, banged the door open at the far end of the commons. "Help! Help!"

Chapter Two

Detective Ryan Greer of the Weippe County Sheriff's Department asked dispatch to repeat the call.

"Suspected homicide at Warner High School," his sister, Cathleen repeated, her voice cracking. Both her boys went to school there.

"Was it a shooting?" he asked, fear for his nephews and Shandra pounded in his chest. The last few years with all the news about school shootings, he'd wondered when one would end up in their laps.

"No. It's a teacher."

"Over." He turned on the lights and siren and drove as fast as his SUV could go on marginally safe streets. The winter snow and ice hadn't completely melted from the roads.

Buses were lined up along the front curb, waiting for the bell to signal the end of the day. He stopped behind the last one, hurrying up the sidewalk and into the main building.

Shandra stood up from a bench along the wall by the office. "I'm so glad you're here."

He pulled her into a hug. "I'm glad you're safe. What happened?"

"I don't know. Ms. Miller found Mr. Huntley behind the Art Quad building." She shivered even though she had on her coat.

"Did you see him?"

Her eyes flashed over his shoulder before she answered. "Not since she found him. There's a city policeman watching over him."

"But you might know something of the cause?"

"I saw something earlier today, but I don't believe…"

"That the person you saw with the man could have done it." He knew Shandra too well. They'd worked together on nearly a dozen murders, and he could tell when she was covering for someone she felt was innocent.

"We'll talk later." He squeezed her arm.

"You can go through the commons and out that side door." She pointed to a door along the left side of the room.

"You can go home. I'll talk to you there."

She shook her head. "I'll wait."

"Direct the M.E. and ambulance this way, then."

Shandra nodded and sat back down.

Ryan strode across the large common area to a door that was propped open. He spotted the local cop and a man and woman standing with him.

"Stanley," Ryan said, nodding to the Warner Police sergeant.

"Greer. I figured they'd send our detective." Stanley nodded toward a man slumped against the back of the Art Quad building.

"Foster is on vacation. You get me." Ryan pulled out his notebook. "And you are?" he asked the man and woman.

"Russ Pawner, Principal," the visibly shaken man said.

"Gertrude Miller. Media Center instructor." She had her arms wrapped around her body, hugging her winter coat tight. "I found him."

Ryan nodded. "Mr. Pawner, you may go. Make sure no

students come back here." He turned his attention to Ms. Miller. "How did you find him?"

She pointed. "Just like that."

"Why were you back here?"

"Oh! My rooms are in the back of the building. It's faster for me to come out of the commons through that door and to this back door to get to my rooms."

"Where were you coming from?" he asked.

"Coming from? The main building." She blinked at him.

"What were you doing in the main building?"

"Oh! I'd run in to check my inbox. I've been expecting a notice about a contest my students are entering. I was hoping I could give them good news and had run into the office after class started."

"Did you see anyone on your way to or from your room?" Ryan noted there were several muddy prints on the sidewalk.

"No. I didn't see anyone." She glanced at the victim and then back at him. "But he could have been there when I went into the building. I didn't look behind me as I hurried into the office."

He nodded. "You can go back to work, but please remain after school is let out in case I have any more questions."

She nodded and started to walk to the back door.

"Please use the front entrance and don't allow any students to come out this way when class lets out."

"Of course." She tiptoed through the mud and snow patches to the front of the building.

"Why don't you wait for the M.E. and direct them back here instead of going through the main building," he said to the man standing guard.

Stanley nodded and headed to the parking area.

Ryan pulled his camera out of his backpack and began snapping photos as he worked his way toward the victim. The man didn't have a coat on, suggesting he had stepped out to either hurry to the office, like the woman who found him, or he was called out the back door for some reason. The cause of death appeared to be blunt force trauma to the head. There were strands of hair and blood on the wall at the point of contact. The large pool of red on the snow around his body indicated it was either a head wound, or someone had cut the carotid artery in his neck.

Pulling on gloves, Ryan checked the man's neck. Nothing severed. The body collapsed in a way that didn't indicate the victim had tried to stop a fall. He picked up the man's hands. There weren't any scrapes, ice, or dirt to indicate the victim put his hands out to keep from hitting the ground. From the way the body slumped sideways against the building, his feet could have gone out from under him and he fell. But there should have been scrapes on his hands or his shoes.

He wasn't convinced this had been an accident. But they would know for sure after an autopsy. Ryan snapped photos up close and on the ground around the body. Sparkles on the sidewalk caught his attention. Glitter. He picked some up on the end of his gloved finger and put it into an evidence bag. Then he scraped hair and blood samples from the wall into an evidence jar.

Having presided over many homicides and accidental deaths, Ryan was leaning toward this being a homicide. It didn't look to him as if the victim had fallen of his own accord.

Had the shove that caused him to hit his head been accidental, provoked, or intentional? This was the part of his job he relished. Finding the clues that pieced the homicide together.

He took more photos, pulled out the man's wallet, and wrote down all the information.

Sirens became louder and died.

The sound of a gurney and voices grew near.

Chapter Three

Shandra sat still as the bell rang and the students hurried out the main entrance. Once the hall and common room had cleared, she went in search of Nancy. She found the woman in her small office, rubbing her temples.

A quiet knock on the door frame caught the woman's attention.

"Shandra. Come in." Nancy began stacking folders on her desk, avoiding eye contact.

"Did you hear? Gertrude found Roger Huntley—"

"I heard. It's awful to have had that happen at the school, but I can understand someone losing their cool with that man." The anger she'd witnessed in the woman before resurfaced.

Shandra stared at her friend. "We don't know it wasn't

an accident. The sidewalks around here have been slippery lately." She hoped it was an accident. If Ryan thought it was anything else, he'd go after Boyd and Travis. She had a gut feeling the two had nothing to do with the teacher's death.

"Yes. I'm sorry. I shouldn't jump to conclusions just because the man was disliked." Nancy still didn't meet her gaze.

"I was wondering if you found out what Mr. Huntley had said to Travis and if he was feeling better by the time school let out?" Shandra sat in the chair directly in front of the messy desk.

The woman looked perplexed. "Travis refused to say what Roger had said to him. But he kept insisting Boyd didn't hurt him. I know Boyd would never hurt Travis."

Shandra had a feeling she knew what Travis meant. "Did you keep Travis in here all last period?"

"On our way here, he stopped at the restroom and I came on to the office. He showed up about fifteen minutes later." Her brown eyes widened. "You don't think…He'd never!"

"No. I don't think Travis hurt Mr. Huntley. But he

might have seen if it was an accident or not." She couldn't believe Boyd would intentionally kill anyone, even when standing up for his brother. "Who else had a problem with Mr. Huntley?"

Nancy waved her hand. "Just about anyone who came in contact with the little prick." She slapped a hand over her mouth. "I-I didn't mean…"

Shandra held up a hand. "I know he came on too strong with the female teachers. What about the male teachers? Why did Mr. Pawner keep him on if he irritated so many others?"

"I honestly don't know why he was still here. I know of four female teachers who reported him for sexual harassment. And I think one student."

Shandra shuddered. She'd had the same problem with an instructor in college. "A student who still goes here?"

Nancy shook her head. "No. It was a couple of years ago. She was a senior at the time. Actually, our star drama student." She tapped a pencil on the desk. "She said Mr. Huntley made advances toward her during a play practice. Her boyfriend backed her up, saying he caught Huntley groping the girl."

Bile rose in Shandra's throat. She hated hearing about these things. Adults were to be safe havens for kids, not predators. She made a note to come early tomorrow and visit with the drama students.

"Thank you. If you hear anything let me know. My fiancé is the detective working the case. I can pass it along to him." Shandra stood and walked to the door.

"Roger was a nasty man, but no one deserves to die before their time," Nancy said as Shandra stepped out of the room.

She agreed.

Walking up the hall, she spotted Ryan entering the commons from the side door. She caught up to him as he stopped at the secretary's desk.

"I'd like to speak with Mr. Pawner now," Ryan said, making eye contact with Shandra.

"He's expecting you, Detective." Rachel reached over and opened the door leading into the school offices. "Shandra, can I help you?"

"She's with me," Ryan said, motioning for her to catch up.

Rachel's eyebrows rose, but she didn't say anything.

Shandra slipped past Ryan and led him down the small hallway to the principal's office. She knocked on the door frame.

Mr. Pawner glanced up. "Come in. Shandra, I'm surprised to see you escorting the police." The principal leaned back in his chair, but his eyes didn't hold the usual merry glint.

"She's with me," Ryan said, again.

Russ glanced between them and straightened in his chair. "I see. Did you determine Roger Huntley's death was an accident?"

Ryan shook his head. "I can't say anything until forensics has a look at him."

Shandra knew that look and tone. Ryan had already determined it wasn't an accident. The thought that someone from this school could have shoved the man hard enough to kill him had the acid in her stomach burning. She pressed a hand to her breast bone.

The principal studied Ryan. "Then it could have been an accident? Do you think he died instantly? I'd hate to think someone could have done something for him if they'd come along sooner."

Shandra didn't understand the principal's interest in whether or not Roger had suffered. As far as she'd seen, the principal didn't have any more love for the art teacher than anyone else.

"Most likely. I'll know more after forensics gets done with him." Ryan pulled out his notepad. "Was Huntley a well-liked teacher?"

Shandra coughed. Both Ryan and Mr. Pawner studied her.

"He hit on every female teacher and didn't take no for an answer," she said.

Ryan faced her. "Why didn't you tell me about him?"

She shrugged. "He seemed harmless."

He frowned and turned back to the principal. "Did any female teachers file complaints against him?"

Mr. Pawner picked up a file. "You'll find all of them in there. Even the one filed by a student."

Ryan's eyebrows rose. "A student? Only one?"

The principal nodded. "Only the one complaint. If the boyfriend hadn't walked in, I doubt it would have been filed."

"Why is that?" Shandra asked.

"Because, unfortunately, most of the girls who come through here know about Mr. Huntley and only take his art class and do drama because that is where their hearts are set. They put up with him to get good grades and good parts."

She stared at the man. "You knew this lecherous man was using his authority to torment girls and you didn't do anything?"

He held up his hands. "He's-was- the grandson of the couple who donated the money for the Art Quad. One of their requirements was that Roger had a lifetime teaching job here." Russ sighed. "I had to look the other way to keep our funding for that building."

Shandra shook her head. It was close to blackmail.

Ryan had been glancing through the file. "I'd like to see all of the teachers who filed complaints."

Mr. Pawner picked up his phone and pushed a button. "Rachel, would you have Ms. Trainor, Ms. Tait, Ms. Miller, and Mary Turpin come to my office please?" He nodded and replaced the phone. "Jennifer in food services also filled out a complaint. But she went home a couple hours ago."

Shandra stared at the man. How could funding for a building be more important than someone feeling safe at work, or in the case of the students, at school?

"There are more complaints in here," Ryan said.

"Those teachers are no longer here."

"I can understand why when you don't back them up in their complaints." Shandra had thought of Mr. Pawner as an upstanding and sympathetic principal. After hearing all of this, she was changing her mind. He was weak and had sacrificed his employees and students for money.

Chapter Four

Ryan could tell that Shandra didn't care for the man's actions. He didn't condone them either. By not standing up to the man's grandparents, he'd put others at risk and possibly caused the man's death.

The phone on the principal's desk buzzed.

"Yes, Rachel? Just a minute." Pawner held the phone and looked at him. "Do you want them to all come back together or one at a time?"

"I'd like them one at a time and in another office." Ryan couldn't imagine the women would talk candidly with him with their superior who ignored their complaints in the room.

Pawner spoke into the phone. "One at a time. Send Ms. Trainor into Mr. Marlow's office. I know he left early this afternoon for a doctor's appointment." He replaced the phone. "Shandra do you know where the athletic director's office is?"

"Yes." She stood and walked to the door.

Ryan followed, feeling her agitation.

In the hall, she turned to him. "Can you believe he ignored these women's claims to keep funding for the school?"

"I don't like it either. I want you to sit in on the questioning. They'll feel more comfortable having another woman present. And one they can tell understands."

She nodded and turned down a hall, stopping in front of a door with the words "Athletic Director Don Marlow" etched on the glass.

Inside sat a slender woman with her blonde hair in a bun. Her back was straight as a yard stick. Her head swiveled as they entered.

"Hi Yvonne. This is Detective Ryan Greer with the Weippe County Sheriff's Department. He's investigating Mr. Huntley's death." Shandra pulled a chair up beside the woman.

"Ms. Trainor." Ryan held out his hand. "This is an

informal questioning to learn about the deceased."

The woman relaxed a bit. "I'm not sure how much help I'll be."

"You work in the Art Quad, so you must have come in contact with Mr. Huntley."

Her nose wrinkled. "Not if I could help it."

Ryan had hoped she'd be more forthcoming. "I have a file with your harassment complaint. Care to fill me in?"

Her eyes narrowed. "He kept the file? I figured because nothing came of my complaint, Mr. Pawner had thrown it in the trash."

"He kept yours and those of several other teachers," Shandra said, drawing the woman's attention. "Even one by a student."

Ms. Trainor shot to her feet. "I knew he had to be bothering the students. He was too much of a pervert not to." She sat down and stared at Shandra. "How much harm did he cause?"

"We're not sure. We just learned all of this," Ryan said, bringing the woman's gaze back to him. "You didn't answer my question. What did he do to you?"

"Comments, backing me into corners, touching me

inappropriately. I caught him following me one evening after I left the grocery store." Her mouth twisted as if she'd bitten down on something distasteful. "That's when I went to the police. But they said I needed to have seen him on more than one occasion and he had to have threatened my life." She narrowed her eyes. "I think he got what he deserved."

Ryan had to agree with her, but it was his job to find out who killed him. "When did you go to the police, before or after you filed this complaint with the principal?"

"After. I thought for sure with my complaint here and seeing him following me, something would be done. But it wasn't. He did stop catching me by myself in the dance studio. I didn't think about it other than I was glad I didn't have to always watch my back."

"Then you think he found a new victim?" Shandra asked.

Ryan studied her. Had the man been harassing her? She hadn't said anything, but he knew she'd been in a similar situation before he met her.

"That's the only thing I could think of." Her hand covered her mouth. "I hope it wasn't a student."

Ryan had the same thoughts.

He dismissed Ms. Trainor and asked her to send in Ms. Miller, the woman who found the body and had registered a complaint.

Shandra stood, pacing the room when the woman left. "I hope that man hadn't turned his attentions on a student."

Ryan put a hand out, stopping her movement. She glanced down at him. "Did he harass you?"

She shook her head. "No. He was obnoxious, having his shirt unbuttoned too much and his gaze hovered on my body instead of my face, but he didn't say anything or do anything that felt threatening. But I was taller than him. These women are all his height or shorter. He was preying on the females he felt superior over."

He had to agree with her pronouncement.

A soft knock on the door revealed the woman he'd found standing with Stanley when he'd arrived.

"Come in, Ms. Miller." Ryan stood, motioning to the empty chair in front of his.

The woman was petite, average looks, mousey brown hair. She scurried in and took the seat, smiling timidly at Shandra.

"Ms. Miller, it's been brought to our attention, you are one of the teachers who filed a complaint against the deceased," Ryan said.

The woman's face blanched at the mention of the complaint. "I thought that had been tossed out when I realized Roger was the grandson of Mr. and Mrs. Dalforth."

"You were willing to forgive his behavior because his grandparents funded the Art Quad?" Shandra asked in a reproachful tone.

"No! I told him if he didn't stop bothering me, I'd tell his grandfather. But I figured that was why Mr. Pawner didn't move forward with it. He prided himself on getting the Art Quad when he took over as principal here." Ms. Miller studied Ryan. "It was an accident, wasn't it?"

"We won't know anything until after the forensic lab finishes their evaluation. I'd like to know everything you can remember about this morning. Particularly any actions of the deceased."

Ms. Miller glanced at Shandra. "I heard his third period class laughing and stopped outside the door. He said something unpleasant to a boy in his class who is challenged. The rest of the class laughed at the boy and he ran out of the classroom."

Shandra couldn't stop the anger bubbling up. That was why Boyd had cornered the nasty little man. "It was about Travis wasn't it?"

"Who is Travis?" Ryan asked.

Here was her dilemma. Shandra was sure Boyd would not have hurt the man on purpose. He was just giving the bully a piece of his own medicine, but to withhold what she knew from Ryan would make his job harder and have her anxious he would find the truth and learn she'd known all along.

"Travis is a young man with Autism. He's in my pottery class and doing really well." She sighed. "I came in the art building after lunch and found Travis's older brother, Boyd, pushing Mr. Huntley up against the wall."

Ms. Miller gasped.

"Why didn't you tell me this earlier?" Ryan accused.

"Because I could tell that Boyd was trying to make Mr. Huntley feel like a victim, like he'd done with Travis. Boyd wouldn't kill anyone." She had to make Ryan realize the boy wasn't a killer.

"You don't know that. You've been around enough

murder investigations to know it can be anyone." Ryan turned his attention to Gertrude. "Did you see Boyd or Travis when you went into the commons?"

The teacher shook her head. "I didn't see anyone until I got to the office."

"Who was in the office?"

Shandra understood by Ryan's questions and his lack of eye contact with her, that he was upset.

Gertrude stared at the wall across from her as she thought about the question. "Rachel, Nancy, Mr. Shepard."

"Rachel is the secretary at the desk," Shandra said, filling Ryan in. "Nancy would be Ms. Tait, who had a complaint as well. Mr. Shepard is one of the custodians."

Ryan jotted all this down in his notepad before glancing up at the teacher. "Do you have anything else you can think of? Any other times you saw someone talking with the deceased? Or anyone hanging around the Art Quad who usually didn't?"

"No…" Gertrude shook her head.

"Why did you register a complaint about Mr. Huntley with your principal?"

Shandra wanted to reach over and tug on Ryan's coat

sleeve to get his attention and show her unhappiness at his blunt questioning. But she knew that wouldn't help matters.

"Because he would catch me in the media room alone and would get into my bubble until I'd find myself backed into a corner. He'd say things that made me uncomfortable and even skimmed his hand over my breast once." She shuddered. "And I think he followed me home one Saturday after I'd been shopping. I had the feeling someone was watching. I kept looking and thought I spotted him sitting in a car across the street from my house." She scowled. "That was creepy."

"Did you ever see him make the same advances on a student?" Shandra couldn't stay out of this, worrying young women may have been exposed to the man's disgusting ways.

"Once or twice he had a student cornered like he'd done with me. I'd get his attention and wave them away."

"Did you tell Mr. Pawner about it?" Shandra couldn't believe the woman had let the man get away with bothering the students.

"What good would it have done? Russ didn't believe my allegations against the man, so why would he do anything if I told him about students?"

Shandra sat back in her seat. She had thought this was a caring environment for kids to learn, but she was seeing a seedier side to the school and the teachers, and she didn't like it.

Chapter Five

Ryan dismissed Ms. Miller, asking her to send back Ms. Tait and to round up the custodian. He turned his attention to Shandra as soon as the woman cleared the doorway. "What were you thinking keeping a crucial bit of information from me?"

"I didn't want you jumping on Boyd as the only suspect. As we've seen so far there are many people connected to this school who could have killed Roger. Many with more passionate reasons than the senior basketball star."

He peered into her golden eyes and could see she'd already set her mind to making sure the boy wasn't the killer. She'd wedged her way into many of his investigations and most of the time her gut and her dreams had been correct. But he knew no one was right one hundred percent of the time.

"When I finish here, we are going to have a long talk about all of this over dinner." He'd no sooner finished his sentence than a woman in her thirties with short brown hair and conservative skirt and sweater walked in.

"Ms. Tait, have a seat please." Ryan went through who he was and why he wanted to speak with her. "When was the last time you saw the deceased?"

"I believe it was when I came to Shandra's class to get Travis. We do a kind of debriefing of the day. Find out what he liked that day, what he didn't…" She stopped and glanced at Shandra.

"I already know that Mr. Huntley was rude to the boy and his big brother stood up for him," Ryan said, not giving away more than that.

"Travis was upset, more for his brother than what Roger said to him."

"Why was he worried about his brother?" Ryan ignored Shandra's intake of breath and leaned forward.

"I don't know. He said, Boyd didn't hurt him."

"Hurt who?"

"I don't know. I thought he might have meant Mr. Huntley." Ms. Tait's eyes widened. "No. Boyd would never…"

"Why did you turn in a complaint about Huntley to your principal?" He'd found that by catching the women off guard, they responded with the truth rather than talked around it.

"Because he was a filthy little man who said things that no grown man should say, and he would sneak up on me when no one was around and try to grope me." She shivered. "And one day, I'm sure I saw him watching me while I watered the plants in my apartment window."

Ryan was seeing a pattern to the man's voyeurism. He not only made unwanted advances on the women at school but had made them feel violated at home as well. He had been one perverted piece of work.

"You were in the office when Ms. Miller came in to check her inbox. Do you remember if she appeared flustered or upset?"

"You mean before she found the body?" Ms. Tait asked.

"Yes. Before she returned to the quad and found the

body." Ryan could tell the woman was stalling.

"No. I don't believe she appeared anymore flustered than usual. She always hurried into the office as if she had to get back to her class before chaos erupted."

"She didn't stop and talk with anyone?" Ryan pressed.

Ms. Tait shook her head. "Only 'checking my box' walked to the cubby holes, stared in, and left."

"Thank you. Please send in Ms. Turpin."

"That's Mrs. Turpin," Shandra corrected him.

"Mrs. as in married?"

"Widowed with two kids," Ms. Tait answered.

The woman left.

"I can't believe that man didn't run into trouble before this, the way he harassed everyone," Shandra said.

"Some have a talent for being undetected by authorities. He sounds like one of them. He had rich grandparents who no one wanted to cross and the women all seemed to have forgotten his advances when he moved on to someone else to harass."

A short, ample bodied woman in her forties stood in the doorway. "Nancy said it was my turn?"

"Come in, Mrs. Turpin." Ryan announced who he was

and motioned to the seat all the interviewees had sat in.

When the woman was seated, he asked, "Did you see Mr. Huntley today?"

"No. I work in the math and science area of the school. It's far from the Art Quad."

The way she said it he had a feeling she had requested that area to work. "I see. Is there a reason you are far from the Art Quad? Could it have to do with your complaint against Mr. Huntley for harassment?"

Her face darkened in color. "When I started working here, I asked to work in the Art Quad because I had majored in art history in college before my marriage and two kids. But after having that arrogant little bastard corner me twice in his room and try…" She closed her eyes and straightened her back. "I submitted my complaint, and I was given the job of working where I am now."

Shandra reached over and patted the woman's hand. She understood wanting to get away from the man responsible for making her feel uncomfortable.

"Did anyone in your family know about the complaint?" Ryan asked.

Mrs. Turpin shook her head. "There was no one to tell

other than the principal. I wouldn't discuss that kind of thing with my children."

The woman's son and daughter went to school here.

Shandra studied the woman. "It is something you should discuss with your daughter. As you can see by the number of women Detective Greer has been talking to, this man violated many women's security here at the school. You need to prepare your daughter for what could happen to her someday."

"Everyone you've been calling in here filed a complaint against Mr. Huntley?" The woman's face slackened and her eyes widened.

"Yes. Think what you all could have done if you'd known and banded together to thwart him." If not for the woman's complete surprise, she could have easily pieced together a scenario where the women had worked together to take care of the problem.

Mrs. Turpin's eyes narrowed. "Was he also preying on the female students?"

"We know of one who submitted a complaint, but she graduated a few years ago," Ryan said. "Have you noticed a difference in your daughter?"

"I wouldn't allow her to take any art classes after I discovered the type of man Mr. Huntley was." Mrs. Turpin smoothed the hem of the sweater she wore across her wide thighs.

Shandra was saddened that so many female faculty members knew about the man and had complained, yet he'd remained and probably directed his perverted ways onto the female students. So many adults who didn't push to keep the students safe.

"And you didn't see Mr. Huntley today?" Ryan asked one more time.

"No. I avoided him. I even took the late lunch schedule to avoid him."

"You may go, please send in Mr. Shepard."

Ryan stood, followed the woman to the door, and stopped, staring at a photo of the volleyball state champs from several years earlier. "Why didn't someone get this man out of the school system? Who knows how many girls he groped and said things to."

Shandra's insides twisted. When all of this came out because of Mr. Huntley's death, she was pretty sure there would be someone losing a job.

Chapter Six

Ryan shook hands with the tall, thin man who appeared to be retirement age. "Mr. Shepard. Thank you for coming." He recited his credentials and why he was there.

"If you're going to ask me if I know anything about what happened to that slimy Huntley, I ain't got nothin' to tell, other than it was about time he got what was comin' to him."

That was blunt and to the point. Ryan liked interviewing this type of person. They said what they thought. "You don't think this was an accident?"

The man studied him a minute before shaking his head. "I have my reasons to think otherwise."

"You knew about his harassing female faculty

members?"

"He didn't stop with the women. I chased him away from a few students as well." The man's narrow face glowered with distaste.

"We've been trying to find out about the students. Did you find him bothering one in particular?" Ryan watched the man's forehead gather more wrinkles as he tried to figure out Ryan's questioning.

"Mostly the drama ones. Heard him tell one once that if she was nice to him, she'd have the lead in the play or he'd write her a good recommendation letter for a scholarship." The man wiped his hands on a red rag hanging from his belt loop as if he were trying to rid his hands of the nastiness he talked about.

"Did you ever tell this to the principal?" Ryan asked.

"Every time I seen it."

The custodian was painting an even worse picture of the principal. The man had greatly neglected his duties to his female faculty and students by burying his head in the sand.

"Did you see Mr. Huntley today?" Ryan asked.

"When he showed up this mornin'. He was in a hurry

but stopped long enough to tell me I needed to put more ice melt on the sidewalk. Like he knew my job better than me." The man snorted.

Ryan found this a bit of a coincidence given the teacher could have slipped on the ice and fallen to his death. "Did you see him arguing with anyone today?"

"Today, yesterday, last week. The man couldn't get along with anyone." Mr. Shepard used the red rag to wipe his nose. "I swear, I've seen him arguing with every adult at this school, and some that don't work here, at one time or another."

The man's last comment fueled Ryan's curiosity. "You've seen parents arguing with Huntley?"

"Sure. He was a poor art and drama teacher. You ever seen any of the plays? If you look in the trophy case in the Art Quad, everything but drama and drawing has awards in there." The custodian glanced over at Shandra. "Bet there'll be some in there for pottery after this last quarter."

"Thank you, Mr. Shepard. I just taught the principals of working with clay." Shandra had found the custodian open and helpful her first couple of weeks working at the school. She liked the man and understood his dislike of the deceased teacher.

"Which parents have you seen here lately?" Ryan asked.

The man rubbed a hand over his several days growth of white whiskers, making a rasping sound. "Mr. Shaw, Mrs. Lawrence, Mr. Paulson. That was the last week. Been a few others since the first of the year."

"Any idea what they were arguing about?" Ryan had his pen poised over his notebook.

"I was never close enough to hear, but from the look on their faces, they weren't happy about something." Mr. Shepard reached out tapping Ryan's notepad. "But they all have female students at this school."

Shandra's insides twisted. She'd been a victim of sexual abuse and knew how hard it was to take charge and tell someone about it. If these students had gone to their parents, they weren't victims. They had the strength to get help. She hoped all of them had. The thought Mr. Huntley had been preying on the students as well as his colleagues, brought back memories she'd thought she'd conquered. She squeezed her shaking hands together.

"Do you happen to know the names of the students?"

Ryan wrote down the names as Mr. Shepard spoke.

"There was also Ms. Trainor's boyfriend here once, looking for Mr. Huntley." The man nodded. "I think that was a couple weeks ago."

Shandra glanced at Ryan. Yvonne had made it sound like the harassment had happened a long time ago.

"Thank you, Mr. Shepard. If you hear or think of anything else, I'd appreciate a call." Ryan handed the custodian one of his business cards.

"Glad the guy's gone but will help you find out who did it. Not good for the school having a murderer runnin' loose."

Mr. Shepard's words prickled her skin. The thought there could be a murderer in this school shook her sense of security. She'd come to know all the students who took art classes and a few who didn't. Had one of the students or faculty decided they'd had enough of Mr. Huntley? Would they snap with someone else? The thought didn't settle her fears.

Ryan glanced at the clock on the wall. "Looks like we won't be having dinner together tonight. I'm going to get the address of Jennifer from the kitchen and the families that Mr. Shepard mentioned. It's best I visit them tonight before anyone can come up with alibis."

Shandra nodded, her mind racing through the names and if she knew the female students.

"You aren't going to ask to come along?" Ryan put a hand on her knee.

"Do you want me to?" She wasn't sure she wanted to hear any more accusations of sexual harassment. But then, she wanted the young women to understand it wasn't their fault. She'd make sure they each saw a counselor.

"It might make it less awkward if you were along. The parents may not want to talk to a policeman." He pulled his phone from the holster on his belt. "I'll have Cathleen look and see if anyone took legal action against Huntley."

While he talked on the phone, Shandra walked out the door to the main office. Rachel's desk was empty. She glanced at Mr. Pawner's office. The door was closed but the glow of light lit up the frosted glass in the door.

Ryan joined her.

"Looks like you'll have to get the information from the principal. Rachel is gone for the day." She pointed to the empty desk and shut down computer.

Without a word, Ryan strode down the hall and rapped on the door.

"Come in," Mr. Pawner said in a weary tone.

"I'm going to need addresses for these families." Ryan handed the slip of paper over to the principal.

The man winced and looked up. "This is going to kill my chances of ever getting another job in education."

Ryan shrugged.

Shandra didn't feel the least bit sorry for him. "You should have thought about that before allowing a predator the run of the school."

Mr. Pawner shifted his attention to his computer and pulled up a file. He wrote the names of the parents and the addresses on Ryan's list. Handing the paper over, he said, "I'll turn in my resignation tomorrow."

Shandra nodded. It wouldn't help those who had already been harassed, but it would punish the man for allowing it to happen.

Ryan handed the paper to Shandra. "I'll be back tomorrow with more questions, and I'd like no one to use Mr. Huntley's room until I can go through it."

"I'll lock it up." Mr. Pawner stood, a key ring in his

hand.

Ryan put his hand on Shandra's back, moving her out of the office and the main doors into the darkening evening.

The piles of dirty snow around the parking lot added to her feelings of sorrow. There were more victims than the man who was killed.

"Take your Jeep to the house. I'll pick you up there," Ryan said, leading her to her vehicle. I have to tell the Dalforths their grandson has died."

Shandra studied Ryan. She knew he hated this part of the job. "Do you want me to go with you?"

"No. This is something I need to do in a strictly professional capacity."

"I ordered pizza this morning. I'll pick it up and have it ready when you get home." She would have forgotten about it, if not for the note she'd placed on her steering wheel to pick up the pizza. Of course, she was two hours later than she'd planned.

"That sounds good. It shouldn't take me too long." Ryan closed the door on her and headed back to his SUV parked along the sidewalk at the main entrance.

She started the Jeep and pulled out of the parking lot.

The day had started with so much promise. She'd been looking forward to working on her latest pottery project this evening. Now, she didn't have a single creative thought in her head. Only sorrow in her heart. She picked up the pizza and apologized for being late.

At Ryan's house, she opened the door and was greeted by a big slobbery kiss from Sheba her Shetland pony sized dog. After a treat, the exuberant animal, dashed out the back door to the fenced in yard. She'd been left in the house longer than she was used to.

Shandra turned the oven on and flicked on all the lights. She needed cheer. The large painting of Huckleberry Mountain with the sun sparkling over the snow-covered slopes was a huge improvement over the dogs playing cards that Ryan had left hanging in that spot after buying the house.

Sheba barked at the back door, Shandra let her in then slid the pizza into the oven.

She returned to the couch and stared at the picture. Would this have all come out if she hadn't offered to teach at the school? It would have eventually, but would Mr. Huntley have been killed?

Chapter Seven

Ryan pulled up to the modern nearly four thousand square foot home on the west side of Warner. He remembered the talk when he was in high school of the rich family who had bought the old Gallagher place and were tearing down all the buildings and putting up new.

The three-car garage had what looked to be an apartment over the bays. He stopped in the circular drive in front of the walkway leading to a massive wood door. Walking up the pebbled concrete walk, he studied the well-manicured flower beds with spring flowers beginning to poke up out of the dirt.

He rang the doorbell. Two dogs began a chorus of

yapping.

"Charmaine, Douglas, stop that noise," a woman's voice said, moments before the door opened.

Ryan held up his badge. "I'm Detective Greer with the Weippe County Sheriff's Department. I'm here to speak with Mr. and Mrs. Dalforth."

The two small, white, long-haired dogs began sniffing his feet and pant legs.

"I'm Mrs. Utley, their housekeeper. Come in, I'll see if they are taking visitors."

He stepped into the foyer and before he could say they had to see him, the tap of the woman's shoes faded, and she disappeared.

The two dust mops stayed behind sniffing his pant legs. He knelt and scratched them behind the ears. "You two are smelling Sheba. She would squash you if you tried to play with her."

"Detective, they'll see you in the conservatory." The woman had approached quietly.

Ryan shot to his feet and followed the woman down a short hall and into a warm, moist room filled with plants.

"Mr. and Mrs. Dalforth, Detective Greer," The woman

introduced them and left, the dogs each jumped up on the older couple's laps.

"Detective Greer, why are you visiting us at dinner time?" Mr. Dalforth asked.

"I'm afraid I have some bad news." He studied the two and judged them to be in their late seventies or early eighties.

"Bad news?" Mrs. Dalforth stopped stroking the dog on her lap and studied him. "Does this have to do with why Roger hasn't come home yet?"

"I'm afraid it does. He was found behind the Art Quad this afternoon. He'd hit his head on the wall and…"

"He complained every night that the custodian at the school wouldn't listen to him about the icy walkways." Mrs. Dalforth's face grew red. "We should have that man fired!"

"He didn't fall because of the ice. Someone pushed him. His death is a homicide." Ryan studied the old man. His facial features didn't even twitch.

"Oh my! Dead! Who would want to kill poor Roger?" Mrs. Dalforth's voice rose in pitch.

"Dear, don't get hysterical, the man is only doing his

job." Mr. Dalforth reached across the short distance between their chairs and patted his wife's arm. He stared at Ryan. "Do you know who did it?"

"I'm talking with people and getting a picture of how his day developed. Had he said anything to you about anyone other than the custodian at the school?" Ryan opened his notebook.

Mr. Dalforth shook his head. "Roger enjoyed working at the school. He didn't have much to say about the people he worked with."

"Except that custodian. He seemed to have a run-in with him every week," Mrs. Dalforth added.

Ryan had a feeling it was because Mr. Shepard interrupted his groping of the students. "I'd like to take a look in his room if I may."

"He lives over the garage." Mr. Dalforth picked up a bell and rang it.

The housekeeper entered the room.

"Mrs. Utley, would you take the detective out to Roger's quarters, please." Mr. Dalforth held the woman's gaze for a moment.

"Yes, sir. Follow me, Detective." The woman made an

about-face and headed out of the conservatory.

Ryan fell in step behind her. At the door, Mr. Dalforth called out, "I expect to be kept up to date on what you learn."

Ryan spun about. "From what I've gathered so far, I'm not sure you would appreciate what I've dug up."

The old man nodded. "I would still like a full report."

"That I can do." He continued following the housekeeper down the hall and to a side door that opened on a staircase.

"Roger lived up there." The woman pointed and stood firmly at the door.

"What did you think of the man?" Ryan asked before moving up the stairs.

She glanced back down the hallway. "He was a sex-crazed little prick. I told Mr. Dalforth what I'd discovered while cleaning and how just stepping into that place gave me uneasy feelings. He said I didn't have to clean the rooms."

"I take it Mr. Dalforth knew about his grandson's perverted ways?" This was interesting. And yet, he'd made the provision for his grandson to work at a high school.

"Yes. He'd tried several therapists, but they all gave up within a few months. Mrs. Dalforth doesn't know about any of it. Roger was all she had left of children and grandchildren."

"I'd like the names of the therapists." He handed her a business card. "You can call or email."

The woman nodded and headed back the way they'd come.

Ryan climbed the stairs wondering what he'd encounter. At the top, he opened the door and was hit with the aftermath of a spicy, musky cologne. Stepping inside, he discovered an orderly room. The furniture was more expensive than he could afford on his deputy's salary and more than a teacher could afford. Either the man had a trust fund, or his grandparents had paid for his décor. The artwork had soothing landscape scenes.

He flipped the book on the short kitchen island open with his pen. One page of phone numbers in the front were for a dentist, doctor, and a car dealership. The back was a small date book with nothing written on any of the days. He checked the kitchen cupboards. Cans of soup, cereal, and bread. The refrigerator had milk, beer, cheese, and apples.

It appeared the man ate dinner with his grandparents.

Off the living room was one door. Ryan opened the door and the musky cologne scent intensified. He tried to remember if he'd noticed the scent on the victim as he'd investigated. He didn't remember but the body had been outside for a good hour by the time he came upon it.

Ryan crossed to the window by the bed and opened it. Fresh air would make it easier to stay long enough to check through his bed stands, dresser, closet, and bathroom. Digging through the drawers in the bedroom, he didn't find anything out of the ordinary. The closet had solid bifold doors.

The doors opened to a ten by ten walk in closet. The clothes were slacks, button-up patterned shirts, sweaters, and three suit coats. Shoes stood side by side in a neat line on the floor. There weren't any old shoe boxes or storage boxes on the shelves. He ran a hand along the shelf and didn't even come up with dust. If the housekeeper wasn't cleaning his apartment had Huntley been this fastidious?

He turned to exit the closet and spotted a corner of what looked like a photograph sticking out of the folded doors. Closing the doors revealed photos of the women who'd told him earlier that day they believed Huntley had been stalking them. The proof was taped to the backs of the closet doors.

Ms. Trainor walking out of a grocery store and one of her doing a dance stretch. Ms. Miller carrying grocery bags into her house and her talking animatedly to someone in her class room. The photo was taken a distance back from the classroom door. Ms. Tait watering plants in her apartment window and one of her undressing at another window. There were also photos of female students outside of school and other women who Ryan assumed were the other teachers who had filed complaints and left the school. There was one young woman who must have been Jennifer from the school kitchen. He had a photo of her arching her back in front of an industrial sink.

Ryan pulled out his phone and called dispatch. "Charles, I need a deputy to the Dalforth residence ASAP." He rattled off the address and wandered into the bathroom to see what else he could find. There were four bottles of a high-end men's cologne in the medicine cabinet. An over the counter sleeping aid and aspirin. The man had appeared to be healthy.

The camera! If Huntley took all the photos where was his camera? Ryan started back through the apartment looking everywhere he thought the camera could be hidden. Nothing.

A knock on the door in the kitchen, and Deputy Trapp entered.

"What was the need for a deputy?" Ron asked, eyeballing the tidy kitchen.

"I found evidence that could lead to who killed the school teacher. Stay here while I run down to my SUV and get my camera." Ryan took the stairs two at a time down to his vehicle. He grabbed his forensics backpack and headed back to the apartment. He noted a flicker of a curtain on one of the downstairs windows in the main house.

Trapp was standing in the middle of the living area. "Where did you find evidence? This place is cleaner than my grandmother's antiseptic room at the care center."

Ryan walked into the closet.

Trapp followed.

Closing the doors, he revealed the photos.

Trapp whistled. "That's some harem he's collected."

Ryan clicked pictures of the doors and how the photos

were displayed before he one by one placed them in evidence bags. "Take these back to the station and put someone to work discovering who these women are." He handed the bagged photos of the women he didn't know to Trapp. "And these, can go in the case file. I've met them already and know who they are."

Trapp nodded. "Do you want this place off limits?"

"No. We have all the evidence we need." Ryan didn't like the thought that one of the student's fathers killed the teacher. However, seeing the photos and knowing what he did about the victim, he would have had a hard time controlling his anger if his daughter were being sexually harassed and stalked by Huntley.

~*~

Sheba barked, drawing Shandra out of her thoughts. She hated that the families of so many girls were going to be turned upside down when she and Ryan visited them tonight.

Ryan entered the house. He looked as if he were as lost in thought as she'd been.

"How did it go?" she asked, standing and walking toward the kitchen to retrieve the pizza she'd pulled out of the oven over an hour ago.

"Kind of as I'd expected. The women were right. He had been stalking them. I found photos in his closet."

Shandra stopped at the door into the living room. The pizza in her hands shook as she reined her emotions in. "He had photos of them? Just them or…"

"There were some students and other women." He dropped his jacket on the back of the couch and walked into the kitchen. He returned with a soda and a glass of wine for her.

"Were any of them in compromising poses?" She shuddered to think what would happen to the women and girls' sense of security if they had been photographed doing intimate things.

"Only two. Ms. Tait removing a blouse and a student was naked. The photo was of her backside—head to below the bottom. Not something a father would want to know a pervert like the victim had." Ryan placed the drinks on the end table and sunk down onto the couch.

Shandra slammed the pizza tray onto the coffee table. "If I had known he was that perverted I would have told you about his behavior. I honestly just thought he was a little cockerel trying to get the hens to pay attention to him." She wrung her hands.

"Sit. Eat. We need to go visit the parents who had a run-in with him recently." Ryan grasped her hands and pulled her around the table and onto the couch beside him. He rubbed a thumb across her forehead. "This is dredging up bad memories."

"Yes. But more than that, I worry about the young women that man…" She couldn't believe she hadn't picked up on it when he'd given her the creeps.

"You say he didn't make any advances on you?" Ryan took a sip of his drink, but his gaze remained locked on her face.

"None. Like I said, he came off to me as a wannabe sex symbol, and I knew the kids made comments about him behind his back, but he didn't push any advances on me. And I think it was because I was taller than him and pretty much ignored him. I only made friends with the people I felt I'd keep in touch with after I left."

"How many of the women he harassed are you friends with?"

She studied Ryan. He was wanting to know who all

besides Boyd she was going to champion. Which led her to… "You didn't say anything about going to see Boyd tonight. Are you planning to have him pulled in to the station?" She understood the young man championing his younger brother. Travis had become dear to her in the short time she'd worked with him.

"I requested the whole family be brought to the station to interview."

Chapter Eight

Ryan had waited to make that call until he was driving away from the school and out of Shandra's hearing. He knew she had a soft spot for the brothers and would do everything in her power to help them.

"What about Travis? You can't interview him without someone he knows in the room." Shandra's eyes narrowed as if he were the villain in all of this.

"His parents will be present."

"I can sit in—"

He stopped her with a shake of his head. "No. It's one thing to have you go along when I interview people at home, it's another to have you sit in at the station." He could tell by the way Shandra had leaned away from him, that she needed time to remember she wasn't on the

Sheriff's payroll, even though she'd helped him solve several murders since they'd met.

He picked up the pizza tray and empty beverage containers, carrying them into the kitchen. If he wanted to get more people interviewed tonight, they needed to head out.

Back in the living room, he found Shandra petting Sheba's head and lost in her own thoughts.

He spread the pottery magazines and his gun publications back across the coffee table. A grin slipped across his lips and his chest warmed. He liked sharing this space with Shandra and was getting anxious for their wedding in June.

Shandra slid forward on the couch and shoved her feet into her boots. "We should go before we catch people going to bed."

"I agree. And maybe we can talk about something other than this case while we're driving." While he enjoyed her insights on the cases he caught, he didn't want to make their whole relationship about his work. "How's the vase going you were working on this morning?" He held up her coat.

Shandra's eyes lit up as she slid her arms into the coat and said, "Good. I like the way it's shaping and the idea I have for using horse hair and feathers to give it a unique design."

He studied her. "Horse hair and feathers?"

"I haven't used the process since college, but I've been wanting to add the carbon etchings to my work for a while." She picked up one of the magazines he'd spread on the table and opened it. On the page were photos of pottery with black squiggly lines. "This is what draping horse hair over a red-hot pot will do. It makes carbon lines in the clay." Her eyes gleamed when she met his gaze. "I've been collecting feathers in the forest and will also use them the same way." She flipped a page and there were black images of feathers on a large plate.

"That would look nice on your work."

He plucked the magazine from her hands and headed her toward the door as Shandra told him about the different feathers she'd acquired on walks on Huckleberry Mountain. Her love of the area showed in her words and animated face.

His phone beeped, cutting into the conversation. He

glanced down. The forensic lab in Coeur d'Alene.

"Greer."

"This is Sheila Rickman at the Forensic lab. I've finished the preliminary examination of your victim. Blunt force trauma that fractured the temporal bone and developed an epidural hemorrhage. The force in which he hit the wall was substantial. I also found pieces of paint, like you scraped from the building, implanted in his skin, hair, and lacerations. There were no abrasions on his hands that would determine he had tried to break a fall. I sent his clothes down to Jerome. There was glitter on the left side of his clothes and face. The side that appears to be the one he was attacked from. Faint bruising can barely be seen on that side. Preliminary report would be his head was slammed against something hard, by his attacker swinging something at his head."

"Thanks Sheila. I'll look for your detailed report tomorrow." Ryan pulled out his notepad and jotted down what he'd learned so far. He underlined the glitter. That could be the clue that caught their murderer.

"Information on the case?" Shandra asked, stepping out the door.

"Yes." He tucked his notepad back in his pocket and closed the door behind them. "Ready to go talk to people?"

Shandra looked tired, but she nodded and walked out to his SUV.

He followed, opening the door for her. "I know this is dredging up memories you had put behind you. If you want, I can ask a female officer to go with me. You can stay here and rest."

She shook her head. "The man who took advantage of my naïveté is dead. He can't harm me. But knowing Mr. Huntley preyed on the students at Warner High…It has brought up memories I'd rather forget." She slid her arms around his neck. "I want to be there for the girls and women whose sense of security he invaded."

"That's what I love about you. Always thinking about the other person before yourself." He kissed her before stepping away. "Let's go, before it gets too late to talk to everyone."

~*~

At the first house, Shandra wasn't sure how Ryan would explain her coming along. But he introduced her to the Shaws as a teacher at Warner High and he felt her presence while he talked with Vicky would make the student more comfortable.

"Is that cowardly principal finally going to do something about that pervert Mr. Huntley?" Mr. Shaw, a man of about forty, with a balding head, two hundred plus pounds, and an obnoxious voice, asked.

Shandra glanced at Vicky. She looked as if she wanted to hide behind the sofa pillows. Mrs. Shaw was small and frail, like her daughter.

"What would you like him to do?" Ryan asked, not revealing the death of the art teacher.

"Why fire him and press charges. No one tells my daughter she has to allow him to touch her if she wants a part in a play. Why is that man still teaching?" Mr. Shaw's face darkened as his anger escalated.

The louder his voice, the more his daughter and wife seemed to shrink.

"Mr. Shaw? Could you get your wife and daughter a glass of water?" Shandra asked, nodding for Ryan to help.

"Come on, you can tell me more about what you told Principal Pawner while we get the water." Ryan stood, physically moving the man out of the living room.

Shandra turned to the mother and daughter. "Men don't understand how personal saying such things is to a woman."

The two bobbed their heads.

"Vicky, when was the last time Mr. Huntley made you feel uncomfortable?" Shandra waited while the girl glanced at her mother, then the door where her father had disappeared.

"Last week. He cornered me in the Art Quad after school." The girl's humiliation reddened her face and lowered her voice to just above a whisper. "I'd dropped out of drama to avoid him, but I love dancing and didn't want to give it up."

"Did you tell anyone about him bothering you? Ms.Trainor? Mr. Pawner? Your mom or dad?" Shandra noted the mother leaning toward the girl.

"I didn't have to tell anyone. Ms. Trainor caught him. She told me to leave. I hurried out of the building. I don't know what she said to him." Vicky glanced over at her mom. "I left school at noon today. I had a dentist appointment and was glad I'd miss the afterschool instruction with Ms. Trainor." She shrugged. "I love dancing, but not enough to worry about running into Mr. Huntley. I can't concentrate thinking about him lurking around outside the room, waiting for me to come out alone."

Shandra knew that feeling. "You don't have to worry about it anymore. Mr. Huntley was found dead behind the Art Quad this afternoon."

The reactions from the two were visibly different. The mother's eyes and mouth opened in horror while relief softened the daughter's features. Neither one had known about the man's death until now.

Ryan and Mr. Shaw entered the room. The man handed his wife and daughter each a glass of water and studied them.

Shandra glanced at Ryan.

"Thank you for talking with us. If I have any more questions, I'll give you a call." Ryan motioned for Shandra to follow him.

She stood and made eye contact with the women. "Let me know if you need someone to talk with."

The mother nodded. Vicky stared down at the glass in her hand.

Out in the SUV, Ryan turned on the overhead light and pulled out his notebook. "What did you learn?"

She repeated what Vicky had said, and that neither one had known the man was dead.

"I'm pretty sure Mr. Shaw didn't either. He's too much of a windbag to have been able to act surprised if he wasn't." He put the notebook away and headed to the next house.

Shandra knew the young were resilient but being sexually harassed was something that couldn't easily be erased from a subconscious.

Ryan pulled into the driveway of a house in the lower income area of Warner. A late model car and truck sat in the driveway. There were lights on in the house.

"This is the Lawrence's. Mrs. Lawrence confronted Huntley. She's a divorced mother of two. Twins. A boy and a girl." He exited the vehicle and came around opening Shandra's passenger side door.

"If the mother confronted him, you're not going to get her and the daughter separated," Shandra said.

"We'll play it by ear. I might have a man to man with the brother." Ryan led her up the cracked sidewalk to the house.

The yard was tidy. The windows were clean and the front porch, while needing a coat of paint, was sturdy. It appeared Mrs. Lawrence kept things up.

Music and a game show host could be heard behind the door.

Ryan rang the doorbell.

The television sounds lowered but the music continued blaring.

The door opened and a tall woman in her thirties with dark brown hair stood backlit by the indoor lighting.

"We already have a church," she said and started to close the door.

Ryan put out a foot to stop the door and held up his badge. "Detective Ryan Greer with the Weippe County Sheriff's Department."

"Lenny! Get your butt in here!" Mrs. Lawrence opened the door wider. "Come in and tell me what my son has done this time." She shot a glance at Shandra.

"Ms. Higheagle, what are you doing here?" Lana Lawrence asked from her curled position on a worn couch.

"Higheagle? The interim pottery teacher?" Mrs.

Lawrence asked.

Shandra hadn't put the name Lawrence together with Lana. The vivacious red head had been quick to pick up the pottery techniques Shandra had taught the two classes. "Yes, I'm Ms. Higheagle. Lana has been one of my brightest students."

"So, this is about Lana? I don't understand why you needed to bring a policeman…"

"It's the other way around," Ryan said as Lenny, Lana's male lookalike, appeared from the hall.

The teenager stopped in his tracks. It was evident at his young age he already knew how to detect even a plain clothed policeman.

"I didn't do anything, I swear," Lenny said, sidling up beside his mother. He was as tall as her and on the thin side.

"We didn't say you did." Ryan nodded for Shandra to take a seat.

She opted to sit on the couch beside Lana. The girl smiled and appeared to not have a care in the world. Apparently, the mother's intervention had relieved her of Mr. Huntley's advances.

"I'm here to ask you all when was the last time you saw or spoke to Mr. Huntley?" Ryan pulled out his notebook.

"I told you Mr. Huntley was offed at school."

The excitement in Lenny's voice made Shandra's stomach quiver with dread. He was much too happy about the teacher's death.

"Lenny, sit down and shut up." Mrs. Lawrence took the seat on the couch beside Shandra. "I saw him last week. Had a word or two with him about cornering Lana in the Art Quad."

Shandra glanced at Lana. The girl's bottom lip trembled as she tried to hold her smile. "What he did or said was wrong. You were right to tell your mother." Shandra grasped the girl's hand and gave it a squeeze.

"Did he bother you anymore after your mother's visit?" Ryan asked the girl.

She barely shook her head. "He-he…" Lana glanced at her mother. "He called mom a ball bashing bitch when I encountered him outside the pottery room the other day."

Shandra smiled. "You should be glad your mom is. Her standing up to Mr. Huntley saved you from his continued harassment."

Lana giggled.

"I don't care what that coward called me, he shouldn't have been allowed to teach if he said the same things to other students that he said to my daughter." Mrs. Lawrence reached in front of Shandra, patting her daughter's knee.

"But he didn't just bother Lana," Lenny said.

"Who else do you know of?" Ryan asked.

"I saw him groping Ms. Miller. She didn't look happy about it. And he had Vicky Shaw cornered one day." Lenny held up his fingers as if ticking off a list of items.

"He was harassing teachers and students?" Mrs. Lawrence stood. "What is wrong with Principal Pawner?"

"He's resigning," Shandra said.

"He should be strung up!" Mrs. Lawrence exclaimed. "Lenny did you see anyone else? I'm going to get together with the other mothers and get something done about this."

Her son's face turned red.

"Lenny, how did you happen to see so many teachers and students being harassed by Mr. Huntley?" Ryan asked.

Shandra wondered the same thing. It had been a surprise to the other teachers that more than themselves were being targeted.

"I hang out a lot in the Art Quad." He licked his lips.

"He has classes with Ms. Miller in the Media Center," his mother spoke up.

"Classes? As in, more than one?" Shandra knew some of the students took a lot of the classes because they were hoping to go on and work in the arts, such as graphic design, dancers, musicians, and budding artists. But even they were only allowed more than two art classes per trimester.

"I have advanced graphic design, and I assist in intro to graphic design and graphic design." He glanced at his mom. "I plan to get a good job out of high school and help pay the bills."

"So, you're in the Art Quad for three periods a day?" Ryan asked.

"Yeah, and I hang out after school helping Ms. Miller." His cheeks reddened. It appeared the boy had a thing for his media teacher.

"I'd like a list of all the students and teachers you've seen Mr. Huntley harass." Ryan poised his pen above his notebook.

Chapter Nine

Shandra snuggled into Ryan's bed. He'd dropped her off less than thirty minutes ago and headed to the Sheriff's Department to interview the Lange family. She'd accompanied him to the Paulson home. The father had been as irate about his daughter's harassment as Mr. Shaw. But he'd been less dramatic and more thoughtful of his daughter's feelings. They'd heard about Mr. Huntley's death but had believed it to be an accident. That he'd slipped on ice and hit his head. Ryan had left them believing that.

Jennifer, from the kitchen, wasn't home. Her mother said she'd gone out for the evening with her friends.

Shandra patted Sheba's head, running the events of the day over in her mind. The visit to the Lawrence family had her wondering about Lenny. She'd liked Lana from the first day the girl had walked into class. Her brother appeared to be the complete opposite of his twin. And the names he gave Ryan… It was a quarter of the school's female students and a couple of students' mothers.

"I really need to shove this aside and sleep," she said to Sheba as the dog nudged her with her big wet nose.

Using a breathing method her yoga instructor friend had taught her, she drifted off to sleep.

Mr. Huntley appeared in a long hallway. His arms elongated and snaked along the floor, touching the females. Shandra shivered. Grandmother floated along the ceiling of the building, she handed out knives to all the women. They whacked at his arms but everywhere they cut his arms, he grew another hand.

"Ella, this isn't working. How can we stop him?" Shandra pleaded, as one of his hands headed her direction. Ryan stepped in front of her. The hand turned, heading for another woman. "He has to be stopped," Shandra declared.

An inhuman voice said, "He will be." Moments later, Mr. Huntley's body crumpled to the ground and his hands and arms shriveled up.

Shandra woke, trembling. Who had stopped the man? What was Ella telling her? That his tentacles went beyond the school?

~*~

Ryan sat in the interview room with Mr. and Mrs. Lange and Travis. Shandra had told him to interview the younger brother first. To allay his fears for his brother.

"Mr. and Mrs. Lange and Travis, I asked you to come in here tonight, so we can clear up some information I learned while interviewing the teachers at Warner High."

The adults nodded. Travis had yet to look at him.

"I was told that Travis had some trouble with Mr. Huntley—"

"He didn't do it. He didn't do it." The boy started repeating.

"What didn't he do?" Ryan asked.

"He didn't hurt Mr. Huntley. He didn't do it." Travis repeated, staring at the table, his head moving back and forth in a negative manner.

"Who didn't hurt Mr. Huntley?" Ryan asked, moving to get the boy's attention.

"He's been repeating this ever since I picked him up from school," Mrs. Lange said.

"We asked Boyd if he knew anything and he just shrugged," Mr. Lange added.

Ryan could tell he wasn't going to get anywhere with Travis. "Mr. Lange, would you sit in with me as I talk with Boyd?"

"He didn't do it!" Travis said, emphatically.

"I just want to ask him his side of the story," Ryan said to the boy.

"Mrs. Lange, you and Travis can remain in here." Ryan stood, leading the father out into the hall. He faced the man. "Is there anyone Travis might talk to?"

"He just tells things when he's ready, there really isn't any coaxing information out of him. Sometimes if you ask the right question it triggers a response." He raised his hands palm up. "Travis reveals what he wants when his mind and mouth connect."

Ryan nodded, not happy with this information but maybe he could get the older brother to crack. He motioned for Mr. Lange to enter the room across the hall from where they'd just been.

"Dad, can we leave now?" A larger, more alert version of Travis asked when Mr. Lange entered the room.

"Not yet, son. Answer this detective's questions and then we can go." Mr. Lange took a supportive seat next to his son.

Ryan sat down across the table from the two. "Hello, Boyd. I'm Detective Greer. I was called to your school because Mr. Huntley had a fatal fall behind the Art Quad."

The young man's expression became blank at the mention of Mr. Huntley.

"I was wondering if you could tell me if you'd seen the teacher today and when?"

When Boyd didn't appear to want to talk, he added, "You were witnessed holding Mr. Huntley up against a wall in the Art Quad at the end of lunch break."

His face became stormy, his eyes blazed with anger. "He made fun of Travis in front of the art class. Called him a stupid retard. That is no way for a teacher to act."

"You're right, that is no way for a teacher to act. Why didn't you and Travis go to the principal?" Ryan continued to study the young man. So many emotions flit across his face it was like watching a fast-forwarded movie.

"Mr. Pawner didn't listen to the girls who complained about Mr. Huntley touching them or saying things a grownup shouldn't say. Why would he care that the teacher had called my brother a name?" Rage was the only word that described the young man's red face, bulging eyes, and curled lip.

Mr. Lange's face had taken on a ruddier hue at his son's comments. "How had this man continued to teach at the school when he behaved this way?"

"That's one to take up with the principal and the school board. My job is to find out who killed Mr. Huntley." Ryan stared at Boyd.

"You think it was my son?" Mr. Lange nearly came up out of his chair.

"He is the person seen arguing and slamming the teacher against a wall."

Boyd narrowed his eyes. "I wanted to hurt him like he hurt my brother, but Ms. Higheagle came into the quad. I tossed him against the wall and left. After telling Travis everything was okay, I went in the weight room and lifted weights the rest of the day. I didn't want to go to classes. I needed to work off the anger."

"Did anyone see you in the weight room?"

"Mr. Shepard, Mr. Marlow, Lenny Lawrence." He nodded. "I think those were the only people I saw."

"When did you find out about Mr. Huntley?" Ryan wondered how the word spread around the school.

"I was still in the weight room. Oh, Nate Bernley saw me. That's who told me about Huntley." His gaze dropped to his hands. "I couldn't stop grinning when he told me." He glanced at his father. "I know that isn't how I should have felt, but that teacher had been hurting Travis and so many of my friends...."

His father put a hand on Boyd's shoulder and squeezed. "I wish you would have told me all that was going on. I would have gone to the school board."

"Even the teachers felt helpless, what good would a parent saying anything do?" Boyd's comment showed how useless the school felt about anything being done to Mr. Huntley.

"Your father and other parents sitting in on a board meeting could have made Mr. Huntley go away. There is power in numbers."

The boy's gaze flicked to him and then back to his

father.

"You may leave now." Ryan watched the father and son stand and walk out the door together.

He crossed to the door and watched the family be reunited. The brothers hugged, and Travis remained with an arm around Boyd as they walked out of the station.

Ryan wrote down the names of the people Boyd had said had seen him lifting weights. He found it interesting that Lenny had been there considering how much time he spent in the Art Quad.

Chapter Ten

Shandra went to Warner High an hour before school started instead of later morning when her class began. She went straight to Mr. Pawner's office. The man looked as if he hadn't gone home. He still wore yesterday's clothes and his beard was unshaven.

She knocked on the door.

"Ms. Higheagle, you're early." He sank back against his chair.

"I wondered if I could visit with the first period drama class this morning?"

"I have already asked Ms. Tait to talk with the class in the cafeteria. If she doesn't mind you sitting in, I'll not stop it." He scrubbed his hands over his face and asked, "Has Detective Greer discovered the cause of death?"

"He has." She wasn't sure if Ryan wanted her to keep it quiet or not. "He should be here shortly." He'd wanted to run to the Sheriff's Office before coming to the school and going through Mr. Huntley's room. She only knew he wanted to find a camera.

The man nodded and dropped his gaze to the letter sitting on his desk.

Shandra decided there was nothing more to say to him. She wandered out of the office, passing Rachel's empty desk. What time did the secretary usually come in? A glance at the clock showed the buses and students would be arriving soon. Leaving the office area, she turned and headed into the open multi-purpose room.

Nancy entered the cafeteria through the side door. Her arms were crossed over several sheets of paper and her stride said she was on a mission.

Shandra made a straight line for the woman. "Nancy? Nancy!"

The counselor stopped and faced her. "Shandra, what are you doing here so early?"

"I wanted to sit in on the drama class this morning."

The woman studied her. "I thought you were a potter.

Are you some kind of undercover cop or something?"

"No. Detective Greer is my fiancé, and he knows I've dealt with sexual abuse in the past and might be of some help, insight for the women and girls of this school." Shandra fell into step with the woman as she headed down the hall to her office.

"I plan on talking to the students first about losing a teacher so violently, then let the boys go and visit with the girls. You're welcome to sit in on both sessions." Nancy pushed her door open and walked in. The desk was cleared of all the files that had been stacked there the day before.

"Did Mr. Huntley only teach two classes? I saw classes in his room every time I was here." Shandra wondered at the efficiency of a teacher only teaching two classes a day.

"First period of the day was intro to drawing, second was home room, then an advanced drawing, and a drama class." Nancy sat down at her desk. "The students in all three classes were barely thirty in number. We decided to do a school wide assembly on grief and then a smaller assembly with just the female students from his classes."

"Do you think it is wise to single out the female students from his classes?" Shandra studied the woman.

"I would have preferred talking to them in their regular classes. I'm not sure why Mr. Pawner suggested we do it this way." Nancy picked up a piece of paper.

Shandra knew Mr. Huntley's classroom would be closed until Ryan could discern if there was any evidence in the room.

"Why don't you ask everyone from Mr. Huntley's classes to stay in the cafeteria and you can speak to all of them at once? It would keep the girls from feeling singled out and then let the boys go and get into the subject of harassment." Shandra like the idea of seeing all the students first thing and judge their reactions. Then watch the boys from Mr. Huntley's classes and then the girls.

"I'll suggest that to Mr. Pawner." Her brow wrinkled. "He didn't look very well this morning. I called his wife to let her know I think he spent the night here."

"Does he do that often?" No wonder the man had looked so horrible.

"Never, that I know of. His family is everything to him. I suppose he couldn't face his wife and daughter knowing he'd let that predator remain teaching here."

The lack of compassion in Nancy's tone made Shandra

wonder if the woman was the best person to counsel the students. "How old is his daughter?"

"Callie is a freshman. She goes to the Christian high school." Nancy's gaze landed on her. "Callie is a numbers whiz, she's never set foot in this school. If she had, maybe Roger would have been dealt with the correct way."

Shandra studied the petite woman across the desk from her. She was full of rage at the man who had stalked the school halls and the man who had allowed it. "Maybe a counselor from another school should be pulled in for the talk this morning."

"Do you think I can't do my job?" Nancy asked.

"No. However, you are not going to be able to hide your outrage at what was allowed to happen. I don't think those who were violated will realize your anger is at Mr. Huntley and not them." She nodded to the wall separating Nancy's room from the other Special Education counselor. "Maybe Kathy should run the assembly."

"She hasn't had the experience I have with grief counseling. It's me or Mr. Franklin and he isn't trained in psychology, he's a guidance counselor." Nancy picked up a folder as the first morning bell sounded. "Are you coming to the assembly?"

Shandra didn't like watching train wrecks, but she felt she needed to be at the assembly. "I'm coming."

~*~

Ryan pulled into the Warner High School parking lot and walked straight to the Art Quad. He'd just left the sheriff's department where he'd picked up the list of names of the others in the photos he'd found. All but the naked back photo. Without a face, it was nearly impossible to discover who that photo could be. After visiting the three families last night, he knew three of the names on the list. Vicky Shaw, Lana Lawrence, and Tula Paulson.

The Art Quad was quiet as he entered. His cowboy boots rang out on the tile floor. Passing the rooms, he noted they all had the lights off. The back door still had the crime scene tape as did the deceased's art room. He tried the door and found it locked.

Ryan pulled out his cell phone and dialed the principal. All he heard was a recording about how the secretary was out of the office, please leave a message.

He retraced his steps to the front of the school and entered the front doors. The multipurpose room was filled with students. Teachers stood along the wall with the door leading to the Art Quad. He spotted Shandra first. She stood near the front of the students, her gaze intent on the audience. Ms. Tait was talking about grief.

Mr. Shepard was the closest adult to Ryan. He walked over to the man.

The custodian grunted a hello.

"Mr. Shepard, do you have keys to Mr. Huntley's room?" Ryan asked, keeping his gaze on Shandra. What would she learn and why hadn't she told him she would be here this early?

"I do. I suppose you'd like to take a peek in there?" The man started walking to the front of the building, not waiting for an answer.

Ryan fell into step beside him. They left the main building, walked along the wet sidewalk, and into the art building. "Have you thought of anyone else who might have wanted to harm Mr. Huntley?"

The custodian stopped at the art room door and stared at him. "I'd say just about every female in this school who came in contact with the man and half of their fathers or boyfriends."

Ryan removed one side of the crime scene tape stretched across the door.

Mr. Shepard slipped the key into the lock, twisted, and the door opened. "What do you think you'll find here?" The man stood aside, allowing Ryan to enter the room and flick on the lights.

"I don't know, but I'll know it when I see it."

Shepard laughed. "That's the same mumbo jumbo the detectives on TV say."

"Thanks for letting me in. When you close the door, would you replace the crime scene tape, please?" Ryan noted the man's surprise, but he walked out and closed the door.

He moved to the teacher's desk and pulled out each drawer, searching for a camera, film, or SD cards. There wasn't even a photo in the desk. He moved to the set of file cabinets behind the desk. One drawer contained plays, another books on various drawing methods, the last cabinet had a few folders in the front and a small fanny pack in the back of the drawer.

Ryan took a picture of the pack before taking it out of the drawer. Inside, he found a small, expensive, digital camera with a power zoom lens. He photographed the camera nestled in the pack and then pushed the on button to see what was still on the camera. More dance photos of Ms. Trainor, a provocative photo of Ms. Miller, and the young woman who had been identified as Jennifer Sabo, the kitchen worker. She was smiling at the camera, but the look in her eye was that of someone being forced to smile.

He placed the camera and fanny pack in evidence bags and shoved them into his forensics backpack. He continued around the room, noting the supplies available for the students. There were two large containers of glitter, but not a speck of glitter anywhere outside the containers. He took a photo and placed a sample of each container into evidence bags.

Satisfied he wouldn't find anything else in the room, he wandered out into the hall and removed the crime scene tape. Shandra had told him, a bit reluctantly, where she'd witnessed Boyd slamming the teacher up against the wall. There were posters on the wall for the upcoming play, dance recital, and basketball schedule. Not a flake of glitter in sight.

He returned to the art room. The play was scheduled

for two weeks. Where were the set decorations?

All that he saw in the room were art supplies and drawings that were half finished. He'd need to speak with either Shepard or one of the other staff members. Ryan exited the room and stopped short when a tall woman with a colorful, long, flowing skirt and peasant blouse stood not ten feet from the door with her hands on her hips.

"What are you doing skulking around in the Art Quad?" the woman asked.

From conversations with Shandra, he had a good idea he knew the woman. "Ms. Tierney, I'm Detective Ryan Greer. I'm here to investigate the death of Roger Huntley."

"How is it you know me, but I have not had the pleasure of meeting you?" She cocked her head to one side, and with her narrow set eyes and pointed nose, she reminded him of a bird.

"My fiancée, Shandra Higheagle, is volunteering at the school in the pottery class. She has told me what a wonderful program you run here." He smiled and noted his flattery had worked.

"I'm glad an artist of her caliber was interested in sharing her talents. Did you find anything interesting in Mr.

Huntley's room?"

"Not really. I'm curious though. The poster over there says there will be a play in two weeks, but I didn't see any evidence of stage props being made." He'd wandered over to the wall with all the posters. Ms. Tierney followed.

"The stage props are made in this back room and stored until they do dress rehearsals." The woman walked over to a door, not far from the back door through which the victim met his death, and opened it. She flicked on a light and the room erupted with color and various shapes and sizes of cardboard and colored scenes.

He noted not far from the door were long wooden poles with long strips of paper covered in glitter. "What are these?"

"The play is '*We The People*', those are large sparklers for the finale." Ms. Tierney walked toward them.

"Stop. Thank you for showing me this room. I need to check it for evidence." He escorted the woman out of the room and began taking photos and placing all the "sparklers" by the door to be transported to forensics.

Chapter Eleven

Shandra was drained by the time her pottery class started. The assembly had been solemn but the lack of restraint by Nancy while talking with the girls had her consoling tearful victims of Mr. Huntley several times. She was pleased when Mr. Pawner interrupted and told those who wanted to go home, they were excused for the rest of the day.

As she walked out of the multi-purpose room with Lana, she glanced over her shoulder and saw the principal giving Nancy an earful. She felt bad for her friend, but at the same time, she should have stepped aside and let someone not so close to the problem handle things.

At the door to the pottery room, she pulled Lana to the side. "You can go home if you want."

The girl shook her head. "I'd be alone there. Here, now that Mr. Huntley is gone, I feel safe."

Shandra gave the girl a quick hug, and they entered the room. She wasn't surprised to see Travis sitting at his pottery wheel, but the scowl on his forehead was unlike the usual expression he had.

"Class, a terrible tragedy happened here yesterday, but we must carry on. You can't let one bad thing ruin your day, your week, your year, your life." She glanced at Lana. The girl nodded.

Having spent the last hour in a group with the students who had been subjected to Mr. Huntley, she now realized she had three in her morning class and two in her afternoon class. She wished these girls had come to her in the beginning.

A knock on the door drew her attention.

Ryan stood outside her room.

She moved to the door and stepped out where she could keep an eye on the class. "Did you find anything?"

"I did. I'm waiting for a deputy to stand guard while I load it in my SUV. I want to take what I've found to Coeur d'Alene myself. I'll be late getting home tonight because I want to stay around and wait for the results."

She could tell by the way his gaze traveled to the room, he was keeping an eye on the kids watching him talk to her.

"Do you suspect one of the students?" She didn't like to think one of the students in this building had felt the need to kill Mr. Huntley.

"I don't want it to be a student, but from what I've found so far, it could very well be." He nodded toward the room. "Be careful, you talking to me could put you in danger."

She shook her head. "Not from my students." But she did a quick scan and noted everyone was watching her talk to Ryan.

"I'm thinking more about the staff. Mr. Shepard was too inquisitive when I searched Huntley's room, and Ms. Tierney was with me when I found what I suspect is the murder weapon."

"You found it?" She lowered her voice. "Where?"

"In the room where they store props. There was glitter on the victim's hair, face, and clothing that didn't hit the wall."

"You think someone used the prop to knock him into the wall? But how would they know it would kill him?"

Ryan shook his head. "I have a feeling while they were premeditated in getting the prop, I think it was more for scaring than actually killing the man. That a blow that substantial would happen is a long shot."

Deputy Trapp entered the building.

"I have to go. I'll call you tonight." Ryan wanted to kiss her but realized they were both working and that wouldn't be professional for either. He turned to Trapp as Shandra returned to her class.

"I think I've found the murder weapon. I need you to remain in the room while I haul them out to my SUV."

Trapp nodded and fell into step beside him. At the prop room, the deputy scanned the items. "You aren't hauling all of this to forensics, are you?"

"No. Just these tall wooden sparklers." Ryan pulled on latex gloves and picked up the first one. "I'll stash this in my vehicle and be right back. Don't allow anyone in the room."

Trapp nodded.

Ryan carried the first prop out of the building and

loaded it into the back of his SUV. He locked the door on the vehicle and returned for the other three props. When he had them all loaded, he thanked Trapp for standing guard and headed to his vehicle.

Mr. Pawner stood by Ryan's Tahoe. "Why did you load those props into your rig?"

"I believe one of them may be the murder weapon." Ryan walked to the door of his vehicle.

"A prop? Are you insinuating that one of the students may have killed Roger?" Pawner's face scrunched up and became a ruddier hue.

"I'm not insinuating anything. I'm following the clues. They led me to the prop room and these props." He opened his door. "I have to get this to Coeur d'Alene." He slid behind the steering wheel and closed the door. This was the first time that the principal had shown any interest in the investigation. Which led Ryan to add him to the list of possibilities.

~*~

Shandra finished the day at her usual time. Both classes had been subdued as well as the cafeteria during lunch. It appeared while Mr. Huntley being gone was a relief to those he'd victimized, however, his death had put a cloak over the school.

She tidied up the room. As she walked by the student's projects sitting on the shelves, she stopped and stared. Travis's lop-sided bowl now looked like a head with one side cracked open. She sucked in air. Had Travis seen the body? But when? And how? Did he also see who hit Mr. Huntley?

Travis could be a witness.

She picked up his clay, settling it in a box gingerly to not allow the piece to collapse. With the box under her arm, she picked up her coat and purse and headed to the main building and the office. She needed to get the Lange's address.

Ms. Miller was whispering over the window to Rachel.

"I can't believe it's taking so long for the police to figure this out," Gertrude whispered.

"It's because so many people wanted him dead," Rachel said matter-of-factly.

"Rachel, I was wondering if you could give me the Lange's address, please." Shandra's words made Gertrude jump back from the window and Rachel pick up papers.

"Why do you need to see them at home? You can call them in for a consult." Rachel stacked the papers and stared at her.

"I'd prefer to speak with them at home. It will make Travis more comfortable." She'd placed the box in her Jeep before coming to the office. She didn't want anyone to think she suspected Travis.

"He was acting strange yesterday. Do you think he saw something?" Gertrude asked.

"No, I have some questions about his motor skills that pertain to molding clay." A little white lie was better than getting any rumors floating around.

Rachel clicked keys on the computer then wrote on a sticky-pad. "Here you go."

"Thank you." She turned to leave.

"But why didn't you have this discussion at the beginning of the quarter instead of now?" The accusation in the secretary's voice wasn't lost to Shandra.

She spun around. "Because I believe the class is helping his motor skills and it is something he needs to keep doing." She pushed on the doors and exited the school.

It was as if the secretary was trying to put the blame on Travis. Shandra hoped to make him the hero.

~*~

Ryan handed the four giant sparklers over to the technician in charge of his case. "I'll be in town when you get the results, give me a call."

He knew it would take a couple hours, which would give him enough time to visit his little sister, Bridget, and her three children. While he'd attended more family functions since he and Shandra became engaged, he was still hesitant to hang out too much or make it a routine. In his line of work, he would always have to be careful when it came to his family.

Within twenty minutes he stood on his sister's doorstep, ringing the bell.

Darla, the middle child answered the door. "Uncle Ryan!" she shrieked and catapulted into his arms.

"Hey, Darla. Why are you answering the door instead of Mommy?" He'd given his sister the stranger at the door speech enough times she should have it tattooed to her brain.

"Mommy don't feel good." The little girl's smile

turned into a frown and she wiggled to get loose.

Ryan put her down and shut the door before following the little tornado's wake down the hall to the master bedroom.

Wally, the three-year-old, sat on the bed, pulling tissues out of a box. Bridget had her eyes closed. Her breathing was raspy.

"Hey, sis."

Her eyes slowly opened. "Hey."

"How long have you been like this? Where's Wallace? Why didn't you call mom?" Ryan reached out and touched her forehead. It was hotter than a microwaved cup.

"If I called mom, she'd think I'm not a good mother. She never had anyone come help her out when she was sick." Bridget started coughing.

Ryan picked up Wally and backed away. "Darla, take Wally in your room and play with him." It was probably too late but if he could keep the kids from getting sick it would make Bridget's recovery easier.

"He pulls the heads off my Barbies." Darla shoved her hands on her hips and looked so much like her mother at that age, Ryan couldn't help but grin.

"You think it's funny he pulls their heads off?"

"No. You reminded me of someone we both know." He glanced over at his head-strong younger sister. She was pale and wheezing. "Take him to his room then."

"But all he has is baby toys." The bottom lip came out in the perfect pout.

"You only have to play with him until Grammy gets here."

Darla whooped and dragged her younger brother out of the room.

"Where's Wallace?" he asked, again.

"Out of town this week." Bridget managed between coughing fits.

The doorbell rang.

"I'll get it!" yelled Darla.

He stuck his hand out, stopping the child's sprint down the hall. "No, you won't." He glared at Bridget. "You have to get through to them not to answer the door."

"It's Sheila."

"You don't know that for sure. It wasn't Sheila when I came." He turned Darla back to the bedrooms and walked down the hallway and across the living room to the front door. He opened the door and there stood his seven-year-old niece grinning at him with two missing teeth.

"Uncle Ryan! I knew you were here. I saw your car." She walked in and dropped her backpack and coat on the floor beside the hall tree.

"Why don't you go make a snack while I call Grammy."

She gave him a thumbs up and skipped down the hallway.

He picked up the items she'd plopped on the floor, hanging them from hooks and pulled out his phone.

"Ryan what a pleasant surprise. Are you and Shandra coming to Sunday dinner?" His mom was always trying to get them to family functions.

"No. I need your help, well rather—"

"Is something wrong with Shandra?" she interrupted.

"No. She's fine. It's Bridget. I came by to say 'hi' while I was in town and she's so sick she can't…" He stepped into the kitchen and couldn't believe his eyes. Of his two sisters, Bridget was the most like their mom. Fastidious was their middle name. "Holy shit!"

"Ryan! You know I don't—"

"Mom, she needs your help bad. This kitchen looks like a bombed aide camp." He couldn't believe that three little kids could make this much mess.

"I'll be there in two hours. Do you have time to stick around that long?" He heard her opening a closet door.

"Yes. I'm waiting for evidence from the Forensic Lab." He rubbed a hand over his face. He'd never been the sympathetic brother. Now it was his turn to show his sister that side of him.

Chapter Twelve

Shandra went home, fed and walked Sheba, and ate a small meal, waiting for seven o'clock to roll around. She didn't want to show up and ruin the Langes' dinner and hoped that seven was a good time.

Ryan had texted her about finding Bridget in bed and sending for his mother. She smiled. He would be a thoughtful husband. The last she'd heard from him, he was still in Coeur d'Alene waiting. She hadn't mentioned discovering the clay figure Travis had made or her plan to visit the Lange family.

"Want to come along?" she asked Sheba as she pulled on her coat.

A soft woof and wagging tail was a definite, yes.

"Come on then." She picked up her purse and the box

holding the clay and headed to the door. Sheba waited patiently.

Shandra locked the door behind them and used the key fob to unlock her Jeep. She let Sheba into the back seat and slid in the driver's side, placing the box and her purse on the passenger seat. She'd looked up the address on her phone while waiting and had a good idea of where the family lived.

Backing out of the drive, she noticed a vehicle down the street when the lights flicked on. Not unusual. People didn't sit around at home. Especially in this small neighborhood that seemed to be made up mostly of single people who wanted to own a home rather than rent.

She pointed the Jeep towards the main road and continued. Following the directions she'd written down, she parked in front of a nice home in a neighborhood not far from where Ryan's sister, Cathleen, and her family lived.

"Stay." She rolled the windows down six inches to keep them from fogging up from Sheba's breath and body heat. "I won't be long." She patted Sheba on the head.

With her purse on her shoulder and the box under her

arm, she strode up the sidewalk, taking in the nice yard, new paint on the house, and the nice drapes in the windows. She drew in a breath, rehearsed her words, and rang the doorbell.

Footsteps sounded on the other side of the door, seconds before it opened.

"Hello?" Mrs. Lange asked.

"Mrs. Lange, I'm Shandra Higheagle, from the school."

"Oh yes. You are volunteering in the pottery classes." She stepped back, her gaze on the box under Shandra's arm. "Why have you come to see us?"

Shandra stepped into the house. "I wanted to talk with your family." She grasped the box with two hands. "I think Travis knows who killed Mr. Huntley."

Mrs. Lange closed the door and stared at her. "Why would you think such a thing?"

"Can you call your family together. I want to show you all something." Shandra didn't like upsetting the woman, but Travis was a part of getting to the truth.

"Come into the dining room. I've cleared the dishes from dinner."

Shandra followed the woman through an impressive living room and into a dining room with matching hutch, table and chairs, and buffet. It was a picture out of a furniture magazine.

"Have a seat. I'll get the boys."

Shandra nodded, set the box on the table, and removed her coat. On the china hutch were two photos of the brothers when they were toddlers. One of Boyd and Travis and one of just Boyd. She smiled. Even at the young age in the photos she could tell they were close. Boyd had his arm around his brother's neck and Travis had his arm about Boyd's waist. They both had big smiles and mischief in their eyes.

Mr. Lange entered the dining room. "Ms. Higheagle, my wife says you wish to talk with the whole family?"

Shandra moved to stand behind the chair where she'd placed the box. "I do. I found something after the class had left for the day and I think it will help the police find the killer, but I wanted to discuss it with Travis first."

The tall broad-shouldered man with graying temples stared at her. His brow wrinkled, and he moved to the seat at the head of the table.

Mrs. Lange entered with the boys. Boyd scowled at her and Travis had a perplexed expression on his face.

"Please have a seat," Shandra said, taking the one in front of her.

"Why are you allowing her in here? She's the cop's girlfriend," Boyd said.

Mr. and Mrs. Lange peered at her.

"Detective Greer is my fiancé. But that isn't the reason I'm here." She opened the flaps on the box slowly as she continued. "All quarter Travis has been working on building a bowl for his mother. It took a lot of concentration and learning how fragile the clay was to finally see the sides of the bowl growing. I think with more practice, he'll be a fine potter." She smiled at Travis and he grinned back. "Today when I was getting ready to leave, I walked by the cubby holes where the students store their work and I discovered this in Travis's cubby."

She reached into the box and pulled out the bashed in head made out of clay.

"My word!" Mrs. Lange exclaimed.

Mr. Lange leaned forward studying the piece. "Travis made this?"

"That's what I wanted to ask him. If he did, I have a feeling he saw who killed Mr. Huntley." Shandra glanced at Boyd, whose chin had dropped, leaving his mouth open.

She shifted her attention to Travis. "Did you make this in class today?"

He reached out as if to touch the dent in the head, then pulled his hand back.

"Travis did you see who hit Mr. Huntley yesterday? Is that how you know his head was hurt?" Shandra watched the young man. His gaze flicked to his parents, his brother, and back to the head.

"I didn't."

"You didn't see who hit Mr. Huntley?" she asked softly.

He pointed to the clay. "I didn't."

"He's saying he didn't make that," Boyd intervened.

She studied the older brother. "Did he tell you he saw who hurt Mr. Huntley?"

"He didn't see anything. Someone is playing a bad joke by making you think Travis did that." Boyd nodded toward the clay.

This was the second time she'd witnessed the anger

and protectiveness Boyd had for his brother.

"Any ideas who or why?" She placed the clay back in the box and Travis's agitation lessened.

Boyd shrugged.

"I'm not here to get Travis in trouble. I want to help. I don't believe he or you had anything to do with Mr. Huntley, but I do feel that Travis may know something. Because if he didn't make that head, then someone did it to make him look guilty. And that person must know that Travis saw something." She glanced at the parents. "Did he say anything that day that made you wonder?"

"It was an unusual day. Harry was late getting home from work, then the deputy arrived and asked us to follow him to the Sheriff's Department," Mrs. Lange said.

"But when you picked up the boys—"

"I only pick up Travis. Boyd has sports after school." The proud mother beamed at her oldest.

"Okay. Then when you picked up Travis what did he say?" Shandra tried to keep her gaze on the whole family, thankfully they had grouped themselves fairly close together.

Mrs. Lange's brow scrunched as she thought back to

the day before.

Shandra gave Travis a friendly smile.

"He said, Boyd didn't do it. I thought he meant rip the strap from his backpack because I had my hand on the strap." She glanced over at Travis. "He was upset. Really upset. It had been quite a while since I'd picked him up from school and he was that upset."

"What usually caused him to be upset?"

"The kids jerking him around and calling him names," Boyd said. "Look, you already know that Huntley made fun of him. Well, the creep grabbed hold of Travis's pack when he tried to leave the room and that's when the strap ripped. Huntley did it."

The anger lighting Boyd's eyes and lowering his voice to a snarl was a side of the young man that made her think he could have easily slammed something into the teacher's head.

"How do you know this?"

"Travis told me. When things go wrong at school he finds me, and we talk." Boyd shrugged. "The teachers let me out of class when Travis shows up. They know I can calm him down."

"Good. What class were you in?" There were already too many suspects to think about, but Travis looking for Boyd could have triggered someone.

"Mr. Lloyd's math class. Travis showed up at the doo—"

"How did he know to find you there?" Travis was high functioning, but she didn't believe he could remember what class his brother was in given the rotating schedule.

"I think he asks at the office or Ms. Tait," Mrs. Lange answered.

Rachel or Nancy would have known about what Roger had done. Was that why Nancy was so upset when Shandra saw her?

She smiled at Travis. "Travis, the day Mr. Huntley ripped your backpack, who told you where to find Boyd?"

He glanced at his brother.

"Go ahead. Ms. Higheagle is trying to help us," Boyd said. "Who told you where to find me?"

She was happy for Boyd's vote of confidence after how belligerent he'd been in the beginning.

"Lenny. Lenny saw it. He stopped me in hall, tell me where to find you." Travis smiled. "Lenny's good man."

Boyd grinned. "Yeah, Lenny is a good man."

Shandra wondered why Lenny hadn't mentioned this the night before. "Thank you, Travis." She returned her attention to Boyd. "How long did you and Travis talk? Because it was after lunch when I spotted you holding Mr. Huntley up against the wall."

"Boyd didn't hurt him!" Travis exclaimed.

"I know. I was there. I know Boyd didn't hurt Mr. Huntley." Shandra smiled at Travis.

"We talked through third period and into lunch. Travis was really upset. He was afraid mom would think he ripped his backpack and he didn't want to go back to Mr. Huntley's class ever again because the kids would laugh at him." The anger resurfaced on the young man's face.

"When you walked out of the Art Quad, where did you go?"

"I told your boyfriend last night." He stared at her.

"You might have told him, but I wasn't a fly on the wall." She returned his stare.

"I went to the weight room and lifted weights the rest of the day."

"You didn't have to go to classes?" He might be a star

athlete, but he shouldn't be above the rules.

"I had classes, but I was too angry to sit through them. If I went home, I wouldn't have been able to practice."

She glanced at the parents. They nodded their heads.

Her phone jingled out a jazz tune.

She ignored it as everyone watched her.

"Back to the clay. Can you think of who might have made the head and left it in Travis's cubby hole?"

Everyone shook their head.

"Okay. I'm happy to hear Travis didn't make the head, but now I'll have to look around in the morning for the bowl he was making." She stood. "Thank you for answering my questions."

"Are you going to tell this to Detective Greer?" Mr. Lange asked.

"Yes. He needs to know there is someone trying to make Travis look like the killer."

Mrs. Lange shot to her feet. "My boy would never do that!"

"I agree. That's why I came here first before showing this to anyone. I wanted to know the truth." Shandra pulled on her coat, picked up her purse and the box, and smiled at the boys. "See you at school tomorrow."

Mr. Lange escorted her to the door. "Thank you for coming to see us first. Travis doesn't have a violent bone in his body. There is no way he could have caused this crime."

"You're welcome. Thank you for letting me talk."

Shandra stepped out the door and headed to the Jeep. It started rocking as she walked closer. Sheba danced around in the back seat showing her excitement at having company.

"Hey girl!" Shandra opened the door and was greeted by a wide, wet tongue.

"Wow, you really missed me. I was only gone for an hour." She pulled her cell phone out of her purse all the while scratching the big furry head shoved between the two front seats.

Ryan. That's who she'd figured had called. She tapped the phone with her finger. Call him back now and have to explain why she didn't answer or wait until she was home with a hot cup of cocoa? That was easy.

She dropped the phone back in her purse and backed out of the drive. Stopping and looking both ways, lights flicked on down the street. She would have thought nothing of it if it hadn't happened once already tonight.

Chapter Thirteen

Ryan had tried to call Shandra when he received the final report and was headed home. He hoped her not answering was because she'd been in the shower. He didn't like to think she could be out asking the wrong person the wrong question.

On the forty-five-minute drive to Warner, he ran the results of the tests over in his mind. The glitter on the props matched that found on the victim. The size and shape of the wood matched the markings in the skin on the side he was hit. From the angle of the marks, the forensic team believed the person handling the prop would have been between five-foot-six and five-foot-eight inches tall. That fit half of the student population. And they believed the blow came from behind. Which led him to wonder if more than one person was involved. Someone to keep the victim distracted and someone to do the dirty work.

He pulled down his street and went on alert. Shandra's Jeep wasn't parked beside his pickup. She'd been home when he called at dinner. He parked behind his pickup and hurried up to the front door. It was locked. That dropped his level of concern a notch. She'd left on her own if the door was locked. Maybe she left a note.

Inside, he flicked on the lights. "Sheba! Sheba!"

Her big slobbery mutt didn't appear. That was a bit of good news as well. The dog may be a coward, but her size was enough to halt most people.

He glanced at the end table, the coffee table, and wandered into the kitchen. No note.

Ryan pulled out his cell phone and hit her speed dial number. The phone rang three times.

"Ryan. Where are you?" Shandra's voice didn't hold her usual bravado.

"Home. Where you should be."

"I've had someone following me the last twenty minutes. I'm about five minutes from the house."

"I'll jog down to Cedar and see if I can get a plate

when they go under the street light." He was out the door before he finished the sentence. Holstering the phone, he took off at a run to the end of the block and then down to the light at the next cross section.

Ryan stepped back into a hedge in case the person following her knew him. Within seconds he spotted Shandra's copper Jeep. She didn't look around, just turned the corner and kept on driving. It didn't take a trained eye to see the car following her. The person wasn't doing a good job of being inconspicuous. He knew that vehicle, but wrote down the plate anyway, just to be sure. He stepped out of the bushes and walked toward home, watching the vehicle to see what it would do.

Shandra pulled into the driveway.

The car parked two houses down from his. Looked like he'd get a chance to ask the driver why he was following Shandra.

Sheba shot out of the Jeep. She woofed and barreled down the sidewalk toward him. The driver gunned the vehicle and took off. The crazy mutt stood on the sidewalk barking at the car as it drove away, not even noticing him.

He'd thought she'd made the dash to greet him.

"Sheba, what was that all about?"

His voice startled the big coward. She yelped and ran back to Shandra who stood on the steps to his house.

Ryan jogged up to the porch.

Sheba cowered behind Shandra until she realized who he was. Then his hand was washed thoroughly by her wash cloth sized tongue.

"Sorry Sheba scared him off. Did you see who it was?" Shandra asked, entering the house.

"I'm pretty sure I know who it is, but I want to look the plate up first." He picked up the backpack with his laptop that he'd dropped on the couch when he first entered the house. Ryan logged in as Shandra wandered into the kitchen.

"You want anything?" she called.

"A glass of water. I picked up a burger and fries at a burger joint and they must have cooked the fries in a vat of salt water." He pulled up the screen to access DMV records and inserted the plate number.

"Here you go." She placed the water on the coffee table and sat down with her own glass.

"Did you go out to dinner? You didn't mention it

earlier."

"No, I ate here. I visited the Langes." She sipped her water.

"Why?" She knew he didn't like her snooping around and with the person following her home… "When did you notice the person following you?"

"When I left here for the Langes, I saw car lights come on when I backed out of the driveway but didn't think much about it. When it happened again when I left the Langes, I decided to drive around and see if the car followed. When it did, I wasn't sure what to do. I didn't want to come home if you weren't here, but I couldn't just keep driving around."

Ryan glanced at his screen. He'd been right. "The car belongs to Deborah Lawrence. Lenny and Lana's mother."

Shandra stared at him. "You think it was her? Why would she follow me?"

"Maybe she's not too sure her kids didn't have something to do with the murder and wants to know what you or I find out." He glanced at the clock. It was too late to go around and ask her. Besides, tracking people down at work to question them usually got him what he wanted quicker. People didn't like their employers seeing them talking with the cops.

"I can't believe Lana would have anything to do with it but Lenny…"

Ryan studied her. "Why did you go to the Langes?"

She told him about finding a clay head in Travis's cubby hole.

"You had a suspicion it had to do with him seeing something, but you didn't wait for me to get home and discuss it?" He closed the computer and stood. When would she understand that doing his work could get her harmed?

"I felt he'd feel less threatened if I showed up," Shandra leaned back against the couch.

He'd witnessed that stubborn tip of her head and determination in her golden eyes before. She would champion the Lange family with every breath she had. He threw up his arms and sat back down.

"Fine. Tell me what you learned?" He picked up his ice water and drank while Shandra relayed someone else had made the clay head and replaced it for Travis's bowl and Lenny had been outside the room after Travis and Mr.

Huntley had the altercation and helped the boy find his brother.

"Lenny seems to pop up a lot when people are questioned about what happened that day." Ryan rubbed a hand over his face. "I'm tired and I still have Jennifer Sabo in the food services to speak with and Mrs. Lawrence tomorrow." He rose. "You ready to turn in?"

"No. Not yet. Go ahead." Shandra had too many things dancing around in her head to fall asleep. Tonight's visit with the Langes only muddied her thoughts more. Who would want to frame Travis for the murder?

~*~

People with hidden faces stood in a circle. Travis and Mr. Huntley were in the middle. Huntley was on the ground and Travis had his ears covered as if the group were chanting something.

Ella swooped down from the sky and plucked Travis from the torment. When the two sat on a cloud, she pointed at Shandra. "What am I to do? That is a mob."

Her grandmother pointed at the group. Shandra turned her attention to the group. Slowly, as if a giant spider started spinning a web, glistening strings appeared from each person and met in the air above the circle.

"Is someone manipulating the students?"

A forceful nudge yanked her from the dream.

Sheba stood beside the couch, whimpering and her tail wagging.

"You think I need to go to bed?" Shandra sat up as the dream raced through her mind one more time. Someone had manipulated everything.

At breakfast, Shandra retold her dream. "I think someone orchestrated the death and is pointing evidence toward Travis. I'll talk with Nancy today and see if I can get a list of the people at the school who haven't been hospitable to him."

"Just be careful. We don't know who it could be. If you nose around too much…" He leaned over and kissed her cheek. "I'd never be able to live with myself if something happened to you because of one of my cases."

"I'll be fine. Besides, you'll be there sometime this morning, won't you? To talk to Jennifer?" Shandra buttered her toast and tossed half the slice to Sheba. Having a large dog made it easier to eat foods she shouldn't. She could take a few bites of the forbidden food and then toss it to her furry companion.

"Yes. I'll head there after I go by the department and fill in Sheriff Oldham. After the school, I'll catch up with Mrs. Lawrence at her work. Someone, somewhere is bound to slip up and give me a detail that will give me a foothold on some information." Ryan set his coffee mug in the sink and stopped beside her. "Please be careful."

Shandra stared into his pleading eyes. He knew her well enough by now to not tell her what to do. But his caring always did more to shake her need to find the truth anyway.

"I'll be careful. I just want to make sure the real killer is found." She hugged Ryan, wondering how she'd been so lucky to have found him.

"Good. We have a wedding to plan for and it's hard to do that without a bride." He kissed the top of her head and walked into the living room.

The wedding! She still needed to get the invitations sent out. In all the hubbub the last week or so, she'd forgotten they were in a box in her suitcase in the bedroom. Sheba rose up off the floor as Shandra headed out of the kitchen. Before she crossed the living room, Sheba woofed and pounced on the door.

"You have to go out the back door." Shandra pivoted toward the kitchen.

Sheba woofed and pounced on the front door again.

Shandra spun around. "You can't go out there unless I watch you."

The dog pounced at the door and dug at the floor.

"Okay. I get the point. You want to go out the front door." Shandra snagged her coat from where it lay across the back of the couch and walked to the door.

Sheba whined and plopped down on her furry butt.

"What is wrong?" Shandra looked out the peephole on the door before opening it. All she spotted were kids headed to school. To avoid one of them getting knocked down by her overgrown puppy, Shandra grabbed the leash by the door and clicked it to the collar.

"Let's go." She opened the door and Sheba refused to move. "You're the one who had to go out this door." Shandra glanced down and found a shoebox.

She shoved back into the house and closed the door.

Phone.

Where had she left her phone this morning? A quick look through the living room and kitchen didn't find it. The second she stepped into the bedroom her gaze landed on the object of her search. She crossed the room, grabbed the cell phone, and hit Ryan's speed dial number.

"You have reached Detective Ryan Greer—"

"Voicemail!" She hung up and dialed the Sheriff's Department.

"Weippe County Sheriff's Department this is Deputy Davis. How may I help you?"

"Cathleen! This is Shandra."

"Hi Shandra. Ryan is in with the Sher—"

"I know. He's not answering his phone. Someone left a shoebox on the front porch." She knew there could be something innocent in the box, but given someone followed her last night, she really didn't need to find a harmful surprise.

"I'll alert Ryan and send a deputy over. Don't touch it and stay to the back of the house."

The line went dead. Shandra held the phone for several minutes before she sank onto the bed and wrapped her arms around Sheba's neck.

Chapter Fourteen

Ryan raced through the streets of Warner, his siren shrieking and his lights flashing. This was why he told Shandra repeatedly to stay out of his cases. She could have been killed if she hadn't seen the box.

He turned onto his street. A deputy and a State Police vehicle had lights flashing in his driveway. He parked on the street and hurried across the lawn. Deputy Speaks walked toward him as Trooper York stood about ten feet back from the box talking on his phone.

"Shandra's fine. She and her dog are in the back yard," Ron said, nodding toward the gate alongside the house.

"Did you get her statement?" The tension that had built in his neck and shoulders eased knowing Shandra was safe.

"She said the dog was making a big deal about wanting

to go out the front door and when she opened it, the box was sitting there. She closed the door and called dispatch when she couldn't get ahold of you." Speaks read from his notepad. "She thinks it may have something to do with the case you're working." One of the deputy's eyebrows raised.

"Did you add that to the notes?" Ryan asked. It was an ongoing conversation at the department about how Ryan closed cases faster when his fiancée was mentioned as instrumental in obtaining information that pertained to the case.

"Only if you give me the okay." Ron grinned.

"I don't care. Is York calling in bomb specialists?" Ryan glanced toward the gate. He really wanted to make sure Shandra was okay but felt an obligation to remain and wait for the state bomb squad.

"Yeah. They're coming from Coeur d'Alene."

"Guess I'll go check on Shandra while we wait. You could go door to door and see if anyone saw who put the box on my porch." Ryan strode across the yard and over to the gate to enter his backyard.

He found Shandra and Sheba huddled together on the back porch step.

Sheba raised her head and woofed.

Shandra's gaze landed on him and she stood. He had his arms wrapped around her before she could say a word.

"Are you okay?" He stared into her eyes. He hadn't expected to see fear but the anger flashing in them had him leaning back.

"I'm fine. We're both fine. But whoever did this better be found. I have never been so scared in my life, or furious." Shandra grasped his coat sleeves. "Sheba must have heard the person leave the box on the porch. That was why she was making such a fuss to get out." Her voice lowered. "If anything had happened to Sheba, that person would be sorry they crossed my path."

Ryan liked Shandra's loyalty to her dog, him, and all of her friends, but he'd never seen her this vehement. "You're both fine. The state bomb squad is on the way. Why don't you go on to the high school? Sheba will be fine out here until the box is taken away. I'll put her in the house then."

As if to punctuate how fine she'd be, Sheba loped to the corner of the yard and slapped a rubber ball around with her feet.

"See. She'll be fine. Do you have what you need?"

Shandra shook her head. "My purse is in the house."

"I'll get it. You stay here." Ryan entered the back door, found the purse on the end table by the couch, and returned to the back yard. "Here you go. Don't let this taint the way you talk to people today." He handed her purse over and tipped her chin up, making her look at him. "You hear me? This is all police stuff. I know it's scary, and I don't blame you for being mad, but you can't accuse everyone you talk to today of putting that box on the porch. You have to let it go."

"I'll do my best." She managed a half smile.

"You're going to have to do better than that. Even a stranger will see through that half-hearted attempt." Ryan leaned closer. "Maybe you need something else to think about." He kissed her.

When her eyes opened, he asked, "Does that help? I can do that every morning until the wedding if it makes your day better."

"Wedding!" She backed away from him and spun toward the house.

"Wait!" He grabbed her arm. "Where are you going?"

"I started to grab the wedding invitations to mail when Sheba wanted out. I'm already two weeks late." She tugged on her arm, but he didn't let go.

"Where are they? I'll mail them when the box is gone." Ryan remained firm about not letting her in the house.

"In my suitcase in the closet. They need stamps."

"I can do that." He made a note to take the invitations to Cathleen to put the stamps on. His family was so excited about the wedding, she'd be in heaven to place stamps on one hundred and fifty envelopes.

"You're sure?"

"Yes. Go to the school. I'll let you know what we find out when I come see Miss Sabo." Ryan walked her to the gate and they both walked through. He escorted her across the yard to her Jeep.

"Do you think it's a bomb?" Shandra's gaze was on the box. That had been her first thought, but now, she wondered if it might not be something else. Wouldn't a bomb have gone off by now? It was an hour or better since it had been placed on the porch.

"We'll know soon. Could be a small pipe bomb meant to go off when you pick it up or it could be nothing."

"Do you think it's related to the case?" Her gut said it was.

"Speaks said you thought it was." Ryan studied her. "Why?"

"If someone had it out for you because of an arrest, they would have planted that when you were home, not after you'd left."

"Unless they wanted to hurt you to hurt me."

The fear in his eyes, told her he worried about that.

"Being a lawman packs a lot of responsibility. For you, your fellow officers, your community, and the people you care about." She put a hand on his cheek. "Don't worry about me. I have many angels looking out for me."

"Go. The bomb squad will be here any minute and you may not be able to leave." Ryan stepped back and shut her car door.

Shandra put the Jeep in reverse and headed to the school. Every fiber of her being said the box had something to do with Mr. Huntley's murder.

~*~

Ryan joined Speaks canvassing the street to see if anyone had seen who left the box. By the time they'd talked to everyone on the block, the bomb squad rolled up. He'd had to call these three Idaho State Police officers before.

"Understand this is your house, Greer," the lead, Lt. Tolmie, said.

"It is. Glad you could get here so quick." Ryan shook the man's hand and they walked to within twenty feet of the porch. He told the man what had transpired.

"Sounds like we need to get an x-ray of the box and see what's inside." Tolmie pivoted and headed back to the vehicle they'd arrived in as one of the other members suited up.

When the man pulled on the helmet a lot like a space helmet, he was handed a small mobile x-ray device. He walked up to within five feet of the porch and held the device in front of the box for several minutes. Backing up, he handed the device off to Tolmie.

The lieutenant walked back to the van they'd arrived in. "Want to see what you have?" he asked, inviting Ryan inside the vehicle.

Ryan climbed in and waited for the information from the device to be read by another apparatus and for the image to come on the screen.

"That looks like a ball nestled in shredded newspaper," Tolmie said. He stuck his head out of the van. "Jones, go open the box. It doesn't look like anything that will explode."

The man in the suit leaned down and flicked the lid off the box. He picked the box up and studied the inside before walking toward them.

Ryan shoved out of the van and met the man half way. It looked like the head Shandra had said she'd found. How did it get in the box? He picked up one of the shredded papers. It appeared to be a printout of an online conversation.

"Speaks, get the lid. This is evidence in the Huntley murder." He glanced over at the bomb squad helping the man out of the suit. "Sorry for the false alarm."

"Hey, we prefer that to someone getting blown up." Tolmie folded the piece of the outfit he'd lifted off the other officer.

The deputy walked over with the lid and looked in the box. "Not much to have made this much of a fuss over."

Ryan agreed, but it mattered to someone that he or

Shandra got this. "Did anyone you talk to on the street see anything?"

"No. It was the time of day when kids are up and down the sidewalks headed to school." Deputy Speaks nodded to the box. "What do you make of that?"

"I think it's a clue to my case." He handed it to Speaks and pulled out his phone, taking photos. Shots from all four sides gave a good view of the clay in the middle of the paper.

"Take that to the department and get someone to try and piece the pages together. They look like an online conversation." He headed to his SUV. "I'll be at the high school questioning an employee."

But before he did that, he'd find Shandra and see if this was the same head she'd said was locked in her Jeep.

Chapter Fifteen

Shandra went straight to Nancy's office when she reached the school. The woman wasn't there.

Backtracking to the administration office, she found Rachel sitting at her desk with a less than hospitable expression on her face.

"Something wrong?" Shandra asked.

The secretary jumped, then shot Shandra a smile. "Oh, numbers. Some months everything lines up perfectly and others…" Rachel hit several keys and asked, "What did you need?"

"I'm looking for Nancy. She's not in her office." Shandra leaned on the counter, hoping for a chance to see what the woman had been working on.

"She has a doctor's appointment this morning and

wasn't coming in until noon." Rachel turned the monitor away from Shandra. "What did you need?"

"Who else on the faculty would know the most about Travis Lange?"

"You could try John Early, his English teacher."

"Thank you." Shandra sauntered away from the office with the uneasy feeling Rachel's gaze was drilling a hole in her back.

She continued down the English and Social Studies departments hallway. The names of the teachers were prominently displayed above the doors. She found Mr. Early's door and knocked. He was a teacher she hadn't met.

"Come in," a deep mature voice called out.

She opened the door and stepped into a room bursting with color. She'd expected words and writings on the walls, not posters of works of art through the ages. "I like your artwork," she said by way of an introduction.

"I'm impressed with your artwork as well, Ms. Higheagle." A man with a shock of white hair, a square face, and compact, average height body held out his hand.

"Thank you, Mr. Early. I hadn't expected to see this in an English room." She shook hands and wandered along the walls taking in the prints.

"I believe even for writing, one must have a palette from which to gather words. By giving my students these iconic images with every color in the world, they can fuel their thoughts with ideas for stories." He remained standing by his desk as she wandered.

"Then you teach creative writing?"

"Along with the more structured practices of grammar and sentence diagraming. What brings you to my room?"

She ended her tour at his desk. "I need to know who are Travis Lange's friends and who are the people who ridicule him."

Mr. Early waved his hand to the table in front of his desk as he sat in his chair.

Shandra sat on the table, waiting.

"Why do you need to know this about Travis?" Mr. Early dug through a pile of folders on his desk.

"Because someone is trying to make the police believe he killed Mr. Huntley." She'd decided there wasn't any time to take things anyway but straight on.

The teacher brought his gaze from the folders to her. "Why would anyone do that? Travis is a good kid. He has some learning disadvantages, but he is very poetic." He held up a folder. "Here, this is the work he has done in my class."

Shandra walked up to the desk and took the folder. She returned to her seat. "Do you know about the trouble he had with Mr. Huntley?"

"He wrote about it in there. He wrote about everything. Who was nice to him, who wasn't. If you want I can make copies for you."

"That would be great. I could give them to the investigating detective." Shandra read the page on top. It was a poem titled, *She Likes Me to My Face*. It was a poem about a girl who liked him when they were together, but he heard her talking mean about him to others. It saddened Shandra's heart and spoke to his forgiveness that at the end, he said she was still a friend because she needed one.

"Are all of his writings like this?" Shandra could see a book of his poems with his illustrations.

"Yes. Open and full of the forgiveness and unharnessed feelings of a child. There's a couple that made me cry. That hasn't happened much over the years." Mr. Early rose, came around the desk, and reached for the folder. "I have a copier here in my room. That way I don't have to walk all the way to the office to make copies. I prefer staying in my department and teaching kids. Hate all the bureaucracy that has seeped into schools." At the copier in the corner, he started the papers and leaned his backside against the machine. "I'm interested in knowing what makes you think someone is throwing Travis to the cops?"

Shandra told him about the trouble the day of Mr. Huntley's death, the clay head she'd found the day before, and her visit with the Langes. The whir and clunk of the copier stopped.

"That does sound incriminating. But I know he would never hurt anyone. Not intentionally." He put the originals in the folder and picked up the copies, carrying them over to her.

"Hopefully, reading these I can discover who might be the person." Shandra took the papers. "Do you have anyone in mind? You've read his poems."

"I don't like to point fingers at students. There are a couple of girls who like Boyd and think his interest in his 'dumb' brother is wrong and want to get his attention. They mentioned if Travis was out of the way, they'd have a chance. There are a handful of boys, who I think feel threatened by Travis. He's an autistic student who excels at certain things and they can't even excel at one thing. Mostly due to their lack of trying, but they don't see it that way. They say mean things and knock him around when classes change. It's like a gang just to hate Travis."

Shandra shook her head. "Do other teachers know this?"

"We have discussed it in the break room. That's why Nancy has started meeting Travis and walking him to classes." Mr. Early glanced at the door. "Class is about to start. You should talk to Nancy. She should have some ideas as well."

"Thank you, I will. And thanks for these." She held up the papers and headed to the door. It had been years since she'd had to swim through students flowing in the halls hurrying to class. She didn't want to get caught in the rapids.

~*~

Ryan went to the pottery class and found the room empty. Unsure where to look for Shandra, he pulled out his phone and dialed her number.

It went to voicemail.

He'd go find Jennifer Sabo in the kitchen and hope Shandra was in her room for third period. Thinking he'd go out the back door, he walked down the hall and stopped. A class was in Mr. Huntley's room. Ms. Tierney was conducting the class. He'd finished processing the room and there wasn't any reason they couldn't conduct classes there.

Strains of classical music came from the dance studio. He peeked through the window in the door and watched the class work on ballet moves. Was the media room just as busy? He crossed the hall and listened. No voices or sounds. Was there a class?

Ryan raised his hand to knock and decided to just open the door, after all it was a public place. With one motion, he opened the door and stepped in. He'd never seen such a variety of electronic equipment in one place. One corner looked like a sound booth, another a filming set. There were banks of computers, printers, and monitors.

He turned to leave and spotted someone hunched over a computer in a corner. It wasn't the teacher. Ryan took two steps in that direction.

"Detective, are you looking for me?" Ms. Miller asked from behind him.

The person on the computer heard her and quickly made the screen go blank.

He spun toward the door. "Yes, I am. I've noticed that between classes there is very little activity in the hallway and no one seems to keep an eye on things. Are there any surveillance cameras set up?"

"Yes. We do have surveillance cameras. But only inside the building, nothing is installed out back of the building." She moved by him and over to her desk.

"I'd like to see the footage from Wednesday." He followed her to the desk, hoping for a better look at the student who was using the computer. But the person had disappeared.

She stared at him. "Now?"

"I can look at it now or you can give it to me and I'll look at it at the station." He wasn't going to budge now. He wanted the feed and he wanted to know who was hiding.

"I have a class coming in soon." She didn't rise from the chair.

"All you have to do is bring it up and I'll watch it, or

give me a copy." He knew it would only take a few minutes for her to do either.

She sighed and stood. "Which do you prefer?"

"A copy. I have another person to question." Ryan followed her to the computers and monitors in a small room the size of a closet. There was a monitor with the hallway showing at that moment. Dance students were slowly leaving the studio. It appeared the camera was above the back door.

He'd positioned himself to keep an eye on the door to the media room. The person he'd been waiting on slipped out the door. Ryan stared at the monitor. A tall, thin person walked to the back door and disappeared. What had they been doing in here alone? And why had the person remained hidden?

Chapter Sixteen

Shandra sat in a corner of the multi-purpose room reading Travis's poems. He saw so much, and yet, forgave even more. While she had several possibilities of who would want Travis to be found guilty, he never used names in the poems. She hoped Nancy would be able to help her discover who the people were.

She glanced up from reading as Ryan stepped through the side door.

"There you are," he said, crossing the vinyl floor.

"What did you find out?" She'd thought about texting Ryan before she started reading but had decided to wait for him to catch up to her.

"Do you still have the clay head?" he asked, rather than answer her.

She studied him uncertain what that had to do with the bomb. "It's still in the box in my Jeep."

He held a hand out to her. "You're sure?"

Shandra grasped his hand and he pulled her to her feet. "Why wouldn't it be there?"

"Because the box on my step had a head like what you described to me and shredded paper of an online conversation." He started to lead her away from the table.

"Wait. I need these papers." She gathered Travis's work together.

"What is that?" Ryan picked up one of the papers.

"Nancy wasn't here to ask her which students had an issue with Travis. I asked Rachel who else might know and she sent me to his English teacher. These are poems Travis wrote in creative writing." She folded the papers and put them in her purse.

"He sees a lot more than you'd think," Ryan said, reading down the page in his hand.

"Yes. And there are several people who he's written about who I could see causing him trouble." She plucked the paper from Ryan's hand and put it with the others.

They walked side-by-side toward the front of the

building.

"Names." Ryan asked, pulling out his notepad.

"I don't know. He never uses names. I'm going to ask Nancy when she arrives after lunch." They stepped out of the building and walked to the teacher parking.

Shandra stopped at her Jeep and pushed the unlock button on her key fob. The locks clicked up and she opened the back, passenger door. The minute she picked up the box she knew it was empty. The weight was too light.

Holding it in one hand, she opened the flaps and found nothing. "It's gone. How?" She peered into Ryan's eyes.

"Did you lock your vehicle after all the chaos last night?" Ryan took the box from her hands and tossed it back into the Jeep.

"I'm sure I did." She thought a minute. "I had to unlock it to get in this morning."

Ryan closed the back door and stepped to the driver's. "See that mark there?" His finger hovered above a scratch about six inches down from the top of the door. "It looks like someone used a wedge to unlock the doors." He pulled out his phone.

"Someone broke into my Jeep to get the head? No one

knew I had it." She stared at Ryan as he asked for a deputy to come dust Shandra's driver's door for fingerprints.

He hung up and studied her. "The Langes knew about the head. Did you tell anyone else what you found?"

She thought back to finding it, carrying it out to the Jeep, and going to the office for the Langes' address. "No. But why would one of the Langes steal it and put it back on your step? I told them I was going to show it to you."

"Maybe it was the person following you. If they knew you picked it up and followed you everywhere to see what you did with it and when you didn't take it in the house thought you weren't going to show me, decided to make sure I saw it." Ryan led her back toward the school building.

"But they didn't put it on your step until you'd left. It doesn't make any sense." She was even more confused than before. The bell buzzed, ending second period.

"I have to get to my class. Will you be here during the lunch hour?" She remained on the sidewalk waiting for an answer as students sifted out of both the main building and the Art Quad, flowing together and passing as they moved to their next class.

"I need to catch Jennifer in food services now, before she gets busy at lunch and then I need some class rosters. If I'm still around where will I find you?" He pushed her hair behind her ear as the last bell rang.

"I have to go. I'll stay in my room." She turned and headed to the Art Quad. This would be the first time since volunteering she wasn't in the room to greet the students.

Ryan watched Shandra hurrying into the building. When she was inside, he returned to the main entrance and straight to the office window.

"Detective, I thought you'd be finished at the school by now," the secretary said.

"I have one more person to question. Could you tell—"

She interrupted him, "Hasn't your girlfriend been telling you all she's asked about around here?"

He glared at the young woman. "What is the quickest route to the kitchen?"

The woman didn't even blush. Her eyes flashed. "That door on the left side of the Math and Science hall."

"Thank you." He strode across the multi-purpose room and straight to the door. He opened it and walked into the middle of chaos.

Metal pans clanged, voices carried, and something whirred. The tang of tomato sauce and yeast hung in the air.

He tapped the first person he came to on the back.

It was a man of about fifty. He glanced over his shoulder, then did a double take. "You shouldn't be in here." he said.

"I'm Detective Greer. I'm looking for Jennifer Sabo." Ryan showed his badge.

"She's in the back. She's the dessert princess." The man nodded deeper into the room.

Ryan continued. He noticed two women, one in her thirties and one near retirement, talking as they put carrots and celery in little paper boats.

A younger woman stood at a counter with her back to the room. With the noise it was easy to walk up and observe her before he caught her attention.

She spread frosting on large pans of cake. Once one pan was frosted, she shook colored sprinkles across the top. When she started to pick up the spatula to spread another one, he tapped her on the shoulder.

"What do you need, Grace?" She caught sight of him

and swung the spatula at his face.

Ryan ducked and held up his badge. "Whoa! I'm Detective Greer. I want to ask you some questions about Mr. Huntley."

Her wide frightened eyes, grew wider. Her rapid breathing blew out in a hiss. "What do you want to know about that creep?" She swung the spatula up and down. "He used to sneak up on me just like that. Only he didn't back up, he'd force me into a corner and…" She plunged the spatula into the frosting and wiped her hands on her apron.

"Grace, I'll be back in five!" she hollered over the noise and nodded for Ryan to follow her.

She walked along the back wall to a door. It opened out into a courtyard between the two hallways. Classroom windows looked out into the courtyard. Benches and picnic tables dotted the pave stone area.

Jennifer sat at the table closest to the kitchen door. "I'm not going to say I'm sorry the creep is dead."

Ryan pulled out his notebook. "I don't expect you to. What I want to know is what you were doing Wednesday between twelve-thirty and one-thirty?"

"I was serving until twelve-thirty and then I went

home. Because I do the desserts, I come in early to get them going and leave after we've finished serving."

"How do you leave the kitchen and go to your car?" While the woman was answering his questions, he could tell she also knew what he was fishing for.

"I leave through this door and walk down to the end of the building and out to the parking lot." She thrummed her fingers on the tables. "I haven't gone anywhere near that art building any day I've worked here."

"How did Mr. Huntley come to be in the kitchen?" Ryan wondered at the man's knack for finding the women alone.

"I don't know how he knew I would be alone the first time he came in. It was early. I'd only been to work for about thirty minutes and I felt a presence behind me. I turned, and he was leering at me. I asked him to leave. He said, that wasn't any way to talk to someone who just wanted to meet me. He kept moving closer and closer and…" Her body shuddered. "It was creepy. Once he touched me, he closed down, and then disappeared. But I marched straight over to the office and filed a harassment complaint, and nothing came of it. He came in several more times, always the same, sneak up on me, back me in a corner and…touch me. Either brush a hand over my breast or rub his, his crotch against me and then disappear. But one night I'm sure I spotted him watching me from his car."

Ryan nodded. He'd learned from the therapists Huntley had seen, he had frotteurism. A sexual disorder. "That seemed to be what he did to all his victims."

She stared at him. "All his victims? You mean I wasn't the only one?"

He hated to admit it, but it was what it was. "Yes."

"And Mr. Pawner did nothing about it? Well applause to the woman who finally did do something about it." Jennifer stood. "I really need to get back to work."

"Why do you think it was a woman who killed him?"

"If there were more women at this school who felt as vulnerable working here as I did, someone must have cracked and decided they weren't going to take it anymore." Jennifer walked back into the kitchen. Ryan stood at the picnic table wondering that same thing. Who out of all the women Huntley had harassed had finally cracked and killed him?

He strolled down the courtyard and turned right, walking along the outside of the school. Did the woman really make this walk even in the middle of winter just to avoid seeing the deceased? He stepped onto the sidewalk and scanned the cars in the parking lot. Two rows back sat the car that had followed Shandra last night. It appeared the Lawrence twins drove the car to school. The one their mother admitted this morning was the kids' car and they used it whenever they wanted. She'd also admitted that Lenny had gone out the night before to visit a friend.

Chapter Seventeen

Shandra sat in her room waiting for Ryan, nibbling on a nut mix she'd packed in case she didn't get lunch, and reading Travis's poems. The boy hadn't been in class today. She wondered if his parents kept him home because of her visit.

She had set aside the three poems that gave her a good feel for the people who harassed him the most at school.

From what she could make of them, it was a girl and two boys. The boys worked together, the girl alone. But some of the descriptions of the girl made her wonder if it might not be a teacher.

A soft knock stole her attention from the poems.

Ms. Tierney stood in her doorway. "May I come in?"

"Yes. This is your room." Shandra placed the three

she'd set aside on the top of the papers and put them in her purse.

The woman had on a colorful flowing caftan today. She would have fit right in at any university or big city but here, in Warner... Shandra wondered what her story was.

"You only have a short time left with us, but I wanted to extend my invitation to you to come back any time. The students have enjoyed learning from someone of your talent and having them hear the same things from someone in the profession rather than a high school teacher shows them I do know what I'm talking about."

Shandra studied the woman. "Do you create pottery at home?"

"I do. But nothing with the creativity you have. I make utilitarian pottery and glaze them with bright splashes of color." The way the woman talked she didn't enjoy what she did.

"Have you tried making something other than plates, bowls, and mugs? You may have a knack for the art side of pottery."

Ms. Tierney shook her head. "I've tried, and nothing comes to me. But I make a good living throwing the dishes and working here."

Ryan walked in. "Excuse me, I can come back."

"No. We're just talking about pottery." Shandra motioned for Ryan to pull up a chair.

"I'll let you two visit." Ms. Tierney faced Ryan. "Have you been snooping around some more?"

Shandra didn't know what that referred to, but Ryan didn't fluster.

"I've been questioning people." He didn't take his seat.

"Are you any closer to finding out who put this shroud of doom over the school?" Ms. Tierney's voice held a touch of disdain.

Shandra wondered where that came from. Surely, she didn't have anything to do with Mr. Huntley's death. The image of the puppet strings in her dream came to her. She studied the woman more closely.

"We are doing our best. I did learn more from the props I took from here yesterday and hope we'll be able to narrow down the suspect pool soon." Ryan flicked a glance toward Shandra.

"I'll keep your invitation in mind," she said by way of letting the woman know she should leave.

The woman nodded Shandra's direction and walked to the door with long strides. At the door, she looked back then disappeared from view.

"Why was she so hostile toward you?" Shandra asked as Ryan sat down and picked at her trail mix.

"She didn't like me finding what could be the murder weapon in the props, I guess." He held up papers. "This is the list of every class on Wednesday and who should have been in which class."

"Why do you need those?" Shandra grasped the one he handed toward her.

"I'm trying to establish where certain suspects were supposed to be when the victim was killed. I find it strange that no one saw anything when I've discovered how many people use that side door to the back of the art building." He glanced up from the papers. "And even more surprising is that there isn't a surveillance camera on that area."

Shandra stared at him. "But there is one in the building."

"I requested Ms. Miller send a copy of Wednesday's surveillance to me, but I haven't received the email yet." Ryan stood. "I guess I should go remind her."

"Did you want me to help you look through these?" Shandra held up the class roster.

He plucked it from her hand. "We'll go through them tonight."

"What a fun way to spend Friday night," she said and smiled.

Ryan placed his hands on the desk and leaned down toward her. "I happen to know you'd rather spend the evening discussing who could have killed Huntley than be wined and dined." He kissed her lips. "But Saturday night, I'm taking you out to dinner."

She laughed. "You know me too well. I'll walk out with you. I need to see if Nancy arrived."

"Why wasn't she here this morning?" Ryan asked, waiting for her to gather her coat and purse.

"Rachel said she had a doctor's appointment and wouldn't be in until after lunch." Shandra walked with Ryan out into the center of the building.

He nodded toward the media room. "I'll talk to you later."

She nodded and headed out the front of the building. Ryan knocked on the media room door.

"Come in," Ms. Miller called out in a distracted tone.

He opened the door and was met by a well-lit room, much different than when he'd been here earlier. The light only made all the equipment and stations look even more intimidating.

"Over here," the teacher called.

Following the sound of her voice, he found the woman in the small room with the surveillance equipment.

"I came to see why you hadn't sent me the surveillance taping."

She startled and scowled. "Because, I can't find it. That whole day seems to have been scrubbed from the memory. I've been trying all lunch hour to find it, so I could send it." She threw up her hands.

"I'll call the forensic lab and see what they need to try and find it." He scrolled through the numbers and dialed.

"Lou, this is Detective Greer of the Weippe County Sheriff's Department." He went on to tell the technician what the problem was and ask what he needed to try and find the imaging. When he wasn't sure what the man was saying, he hit the speaker button. Ms. Miller nodded and started moving about in the closet disconnecting wires and stacking machines.

"And that's what I'll need," Lou ended.

"Thank you. I'll get that to you this afternoon." Ryan hit the off button.

Ms. Miller had the equipment loaded into a cardboard box. "I'll need a receipt from you in case any of this doesn't come back."

Ryan pulled a receipt from his backpack, filled it out, and handed it to the teacher. "I'm glad you knew what Lou was talking about."

She grinned. "I take it you're not a geek."

He shook his head. "I can barely run my phone and my television."

Ms. Miller chuckled. "That's why you and Shandra make a good couple. She's not into this type of thing either."

The bell rang, and students began entering the room.

"You might want to wait until everyone gets in, otherwise you'll be fighting the tide." Ms. Miller closed the surveillance room door and stepped up to her desk.

He watched the kids enter chatting and taking seats in the area that looked like a sound system. While he was intrigued to stick around and watch, he had a killer to catch.

When only a trickle of students entered, he took the chance to leave. In the hall, he headed for Shandra's room. He'd let her know he was making a trip to Coeur d'Alene.

Standing by the door watching her explain a technique to the class, he had an idea. He carried the box out to his vehicle and climbed in. He pulled out his phone and texted Shandra.

I have evidence to take to the Forensics Lab. I'm going to let Sheba out and pack clothes for us. Come home as soon as you're done teaching and we'll spend the night in Coeur d'Alene.

He pulled out of the parking lot. They could leave Sheba at his sister's. The kids loved her, and she loved the kids. They could spend tomorrow doing some of the wedding shopping Shandra had been talking about.

Shandra heard her phone buzz as she walked back to the desk to set down the tools she'd been showing the class. She picked up her phone and read the text. The idea of spending the night away from Warner was appealing. She would have rather gone home, but a night being with Ryan knowing nothing would interrupt would be nice. She texted back a thumbs up. But she hadn't been able to find Nancy in the last half hour of the lunch period.

The class was busy working on their projects.

"Class, I'm going to run to the office. Keep working and I'll be right back." She decided to take the back door and quicker route through the multi-purpose room, much like Gertrude had the day she found Mr. Huntley.

She pushed open the door into the bright sunshine and blinked. The door thunked behind her. Staring forward, concentrating on the door to the main building, she didn't see the area where the body would have been. She did a quick look over her shoulder and was relieved to not find a body. It was easy to see the body could have been against the wall when Gertrude hurried to the office, much like she was doing.

Shandra continued into the school and over to the office.

Rachel had her head tipped down, reading something on her desk.

The imagery she'd read in Travis's poem hit Shandra as she stared at the top of the secretary's head. The deep cherry color could also be construed as red like an apple. The indention of a cowlick on the top of her head with the red hair and she could see the resemblance that Travis had referred to when talking about the female tormenter.

Shandra cleared her throat.

The secretary's head jerked. Rachel's gaze didn't hold welcome. "What do you need?"

"Did Nancy check in?" Shandra had a hard time keeping her thoughts from flowing off her tongue.

"She called in and said she wasn't feeling well enough to come to school. But she'll be in on Monday." Rachel dropped her gaze back to her desk.

Shandra studied the top of the woman's head one more time and headed back to her classroom. What had come over Nancy so quickly? And how did that creature get a job working as a secretary when she had the compassion of a drill sergeant.

Chapter Eighteen

Shandra hurried home and found her suitcase sitting alongside Ryan's duffel bag at the front door along with food and treats for Sheba and the dog's favorite bed.

"It looks like you thought of everything," she said, dropping her purse and coat on the couch and heading to the bathroom to make sure he'd gathered everything she thought she'd need.

Ryan followed her. "Your toiletry bag is sitting there. I wasn't sure what you wanted."

She kissed his cheek. "You are too good to me." As she gathered what she needed, she told him about her discovery of Rachel being the female she believed Travis talked about in his poems.

He pulled out his phone and started talking. "Cathleen,

do a background check on Rachel Taylor, secretary at the high school." He listened. "Only one year? Where did she come from?"

Shandra leaned in trying to hear what his sister said. Cathleen was on the PTA and volunteered at the high school to keep tabs on her two boys.

Ryan hung up. "Rachel has only been the secretary there for one year. The secretary before retired and they had trouble filling the spot until Rachel moved to town and was hired."

"What do you mean moved to town and was hired?" Shandra didn't understand how she'd beat out people who lived here.

"Cathleen said Mr. Pawner showed up at a school board meeting and said the position of secretary had been filled and no one asked any questions. Then they saw who had filled the position and he wouldn't fire her."

Shandra stared at him. "Another case where the principal may have hired her for the wrong reason? Like money?"

"We'll know when we get that background check." Ryan nodded to the bag in her hand. "You ready?"

"I am."

They loaded everything, including the box Ryan was taking to Forensics, into her Jeep and loaded Sheba into the back seat.

She could tell by the dog's excitement, Sheba thought she was going home. Shandra hoped the animal wouldn't be too disappointed when they dropped her off at Bridget's.

Once they were on the highway, Shandra asked, "Why do you need to take that equipment?"

"It's the surveillance equipment. Someone wiped the day Huntley was killed off the memory. Forensics thinks they can get it back or at least enough we might see who took that prop out the back door and brought it back in."

"Who had access to the equipment?" This was beginning to look more and more like a well thought out event rather than a case of emotions taking over.

"From what I saw today, anyone who walked into the media room. For all the equipment that is in that room, I have yet to see it locked. Ms. Miller wasn't in the room earlier today and I walked in. There was someone on a computer, but he wore a hoodie and got out when the teacher arrived, and we were talking. But I could tell, whoever it was didn't want me to see them."

"Could that person have been deleting the files?"

"No. This person wasn't in the surveillance room. He was on a computer in a corner. I tried to watch him on the camera when he left. The hood covered him too well."

Shandra twisted in her seat and studied Ryan as he drove. "You say he. What makes you think it was a male?"

"Tall, slender, jeans, athletic shoes. Long feet for a girl, and the way he walked."

She nodded. "Was he built like Boyd Lange?" This was risky since Ryan believed the boy was his best suspect, but she had to show him, he wasn't the only one.

Ryan glanced at her and grinned. "I know what you're doing, but no, he didn't have wide shoulders like Boyd. And his legs weren't as stout. They were long and thin."

Shandra nodded. The description fit someone who had been slinking around the Art Quad halls a lot lately. "Like Lenny?"

"Yeah, a lot like Lenny." Ryan put a hand on her knee. "How did you come up with that?"

"I've seen a lot of his build lately. He's been lurking in the Art Quad at all times of the day. It's as if he's nervous and wants to say something but is afraid."

"Like he knows something?"

"Could be. I'm not sure." She thought a moment. "Lana doesn't seem any different. In fact, she's even more outgoing with Mr. Huntley gone."

"I imagine there are a lot of girls who are feeling that way." He scowled. "What did Nancy have to say about your thoughts on the poems?"

"I don't know. She never showed up today. Rachel said Nancy called in and said she wouldn't be in after her doctor's appointment. I guess I'll have to wait until Monday to ask her."

They pulled into Coeur d'Alene and Ryan drove straight to the forensic lab. Shandra took Sheba for a walk while Ryan dropped of the box and visited with the technicians working the case.

There was a grassy area with trees to the left of the parking lot. They wandered around and Sheba sniffed all the tree trunks and bushes.

Ryan found them. "Shall we take Sheba to Bridget's?"

Shandra patted the dog's wide head. "Might as well. Then we can find a nice place for dinner."

They drove to the northern side of town and stopped in front of the house. Ryan's mother's car was in the driveway.

"Is Bridget still not feeling well?" Shandra slipped out of her door.

Ryan came around as she let Sheba out of the back. "She's better, but mom has been having so much fun helping she doesn't want to leave."

Shandra laughed. "Poor Bridget. How do you tell your mother to go home, that you no longer need her?"

"I think, that's why she was more than happy to have us come over." Ryan grabbed the box with Sheba's food, treats, toys, and the bed.

The door opened before they reached the porch.

Bridget's middle child, Darla, ran out and wrapped her arms around Sheba's neck. "You're here!"

Sheba licked the girl's arm and wagged her tail. There was no need to worry her dog wouldn't be happy here.

"Hi, Darla. Why don't you lead Sheba into the house," Shandra said, handing the leash to the girl.

Darla released Sheba's neck and took the leash, talking to the dog all the way into the house and it appeared straight into her bedroom.

Shandra laughed, following the two into the house.

Ryan's phone buzzed. He motioned outside and stepped back out on the porch closing the door.

That call couldn't have timed it any better for him to duck out. Colleen Greer sat in a chair while her youngest daughter stood next to it. From the stubborn set to their chins, they had been having a discussion before the arrival of their guests.

"Mrs. Greer, Bridget, it's good to see you both." Shandra entered the living room, drawing the women's attention away from one another.

"Shandra, it's been a long time. You need to talk Ryan into coming to more family dinners," Colleen stood. "I'll get you some tea."

"That's not necessary. We're going to get dinner when we leave here." Shandra glanced toward the door, wondering what could be keeping Ryan. Forensics couldn't have discovered anything this quickly.

"Where are you going to dinner?" Bridget asked.

"I'm not sure. Ryan is in charge." She sent another furtive glance toward the door. "He had a call just as we started in the door."

That same door, opened. Ryan strode in, his face furrowed. "We have to go back to Warner."

Shandra stood. "What happened?"

He grasped her hands. "Nancy Tait's body was found."

Her knees gave way. Ryan settled her down onto the chair.

"Nancy? But I thought she had a doctor's appointment? How?" Shandra's mind raced, trying to figure out what could have happened to her friend.

Ryan knew Shandra had made friends with the counselor at the high school. Seeing her so distraught, he made a vow to find the one who took away the woman's life. "She jumped off the school and landed in the courtyard."

Shandra made a noise between a squeak and a grunt. "No! She wouldn't have jumped. Something's not right."

His mom put a hand on Shandra's shoulder. "Why don't you leave Shandra and Sheba here for the night. I'll bring them back in the morning."

"No. I'm going with Ryan. This isn't right. She wouldn't take her life." Shandra peered into his eyes. "She must have figured out who killed Mr. Huntley."

Ryan wanted to agree, but he'd witnessed the teacher's neurotic behavior even if Shandra hadn't. "We'll know more after an autopsy."

"I'll get Sheba," Shandra stood and walked down the hall to Darla's room.

"You should make her stay here," his mom said.

"I don't make Shandra do anything. If she wants to come back with me that's her business." Ryan walked to the door as Shandra and Sheba emerged from the hallway.

"Where's her box?" Shandra asked.

"I put it back in the Jeep after the call." Ryan opened the door. "Sorry we can't stay." He glanced at Darla's protruding lip. "We'll bring her back for a weekend stay soon. I promise."

"I'm sorry we have to leave so soon." Shandra gave everyone a hug. "We'll be back when this murder gets solved."

He ushered the woman and dog out to the Jeep. It seemed to be a bit of a coincidence that Ms. Tait jumped off a roof after a man she despised was killed. He would have thought she'd have thrown a party. It was clear

Shandra had the same thought.

On the way back to Warner they said very little. The police were waiting for him to arrive to investigate. Without his SUV with siren and lights, he went as fast as he dared with regards to the traffic.

As they entered Warner he said, "I have to switch rigs."

"I'm going with you." Shandra had stated it several times on the ride.

"You aren't a law enforcement officer." He didn't mind her going, but he didn't want to get reamed for bringing a civilian to the scene.

"They don't have to know we stopped at the house first. Everyone knew we were headed to Coeur d'Alene for the night." She pulled her house key out of her purse.

He pulled into the drive. She had Sheba out and into the house before he had his SUV started. Shandra hurried into his passenger seat and clicked the seat belt signaling there was no way he'd get her out.

Ryan turned on the lights and siren and headed to the school.

Chapter Nineteen

Shandra still couldn't believe that Nancy was dead. She stood back watching Ryan give orders and do his investigating. She'd had to do a lot of talking to get him to let her see the crime scene. After she'd agreed to stand back and not say or do anything, he allowed it.

Mr. Shepard stood off to the side, his head bowed. Had he found her? Shandra shuddered. From here she could see enough to know her pretty friend had landed face first.

Ryan took photos and talked to the city policeman who had been questioning Mr. Shepard when they'd arrived. Since then paramedics had appeared and stood to the side waiting with a body bag and gurney. The medical examiner had studied the body and left.

The closed-in courtyard grew dark. Mr. Shepard

disappeared, and lights lit up the benches, picnic tables, and paving stones.

Ryan now worked closer to the body; marking, photographing, and picking up items before placing them in small plastic bags. What was he looking for?

"It's a sad thing," Mr. Shepard said from beside her.

She glanced over at the custodian. "It is. Did-did you see her…"

"No. And I don't believe for a minute she jumped." He glanced around and lowered his voice. "She and Mr. Pawner were going at it this afternoon."

Shandra gave all her attention to Mr. Shepard. "This afternoon? When?"

"Oh, I'd say about two. Yeah, that's when. I came out of the furnace room, it was time to change the filters, and spotted them behind the Art Quad. I could tell the conversation wasn't friendly and ducked into the main building quick as I could." Mr. Shepard dared a glance toward the body. "Guess maybe I should have stepped in."

"But I was told Ms. Tait wasn't coming in this afternoon." Shandra studied the man. "What do you think of Rachel, the secretary?"

"She's sneaky. Not steal things sneaky, but just plain listening in on everything and knowing more than a secretary should."

"But she needs to know everything that happens in the school." Shandra had a suspicion she knew what he meant but wanted him to come out and say it.

"Not school related stuff but personal stuff. Stuff that I'm pretty sure she's been paying for vacations with." Mr. Shepard nodded his head.

"Like a blackmailer?" That was the feeling she'd had as well about the woman.

He put a finger on his nose.

Ryan walked toward them. His gaze took them both in. "What are you discussing over here?"

"The secretary. You said I couldn't talk about what I'm seeing." Shandra smiled.

"Mr. Shepard is this true? You're only talking about the secretary?" Ryan studied the man.

"Yes, sir. We were talking about Miss Rachel." Mr. Shepard nodded.

Ryan glanced between them. "Why?"

"Why were we talking about Miss Rachel?" The older

man acted as if he'd dropped ten IQ points.

Shandra had a hard time not grinning.

Ryan faced her. "Why were you talking about the secretary? Does it have anything to do with my crime scene?"

"She came up in conversation, and we were discussing how neither one of us trusted her. As for if it matters to your crime scene, time will tell." Shandra peered straight into his eyes. She had a strong sense that Rachel was caught up in both deaths.

The EMTs rolled the gurney away with Nancy's body.

"I'm finished here other than taking Mr. Shepard's statement." Ryan nodded to a picnic table not ten feet from them.

They all walked over and sat down.

Ryan pulled out his notepad and poised his pen over it. "Mr. Shepard, would you please tell me how and when you discovered the body?"

The man nodded. "I'd finished up cleaning the Math and Sciences hall and came out to the multi-purpose room for a break. Jerry, he comes in around noon and helps until we leave at six, beeped me on the radio saying he had a spill under a bookcase, could I help him move it. I stood up to go help and saw something fall off the roof in the courtyard. I thought maybe it was a cloth or flag or something. But…" He swallowed. "I could tell as soon as I stepped outside it was a person. When I saw it was Ms. Tait…" He shook his head and tears glistened in his eyes. "Made me wish I'd done something earlier."

Ryan latched onto his words. "Done something earlier? What? Did you see her try to attempt a suicide before?"

The man glared at Ryan. "No! She didn't jump. I can guarantee that. She wouldn't have taken her life."

"Why are you so sure?" Ryan asked.

"Just last week, she told me she and her boyfriend were going on a hike across the UK for summer vacation. She showed me the brochures and I could tell it was something she'd been looking forward to for a long time." Mr. Shepard glanced over at Shandra. "You don't believe she took her own life, do you?"

"No, I don't."

"Then what do you wish you'd have stopped?" Ryan asked, drawing the custodian's attention.

"Mr. Pawner and Ms. Tait were arguing up a storm this

afternoon."

Ryan looked straight at her. "I thought you said Ms. Tait wasn't at school."

"That's what Rachel told me when I asked about her. She said that Nancy had called in after her doctor's appointment and said she wasn't coming in for the rest of the day." Shandra was still fuming that the secretary had lied to her.

Ryan studied the two of them. "Did you see her anywhere other than arguing with Mr. Pawner?"

"No, sir." Mr. Shepard shook his head.

Shandra glanced up at the top of the building. "How does someone get up there?"

Ryan wasn't sure why Shandra had changed the subject, but it was one of the questions he had for the custodian. "I'd like to know the same thing."

"I can take you up there if you want to go." Mr. Shepard stood.

"I do." Ryan walked over to his backpack and shouldered it. "Why don't you stay here," he said to Shandra.

She shook her head. "I'm coming. I want to see this."

He'd expected that reply.

Mr. Shepard led them into the school and to a corner of the two-story, open beam multipurpose room. He unlocked a door onto a set of stairs. "These take us up on the roof of the English/Social Studies wing."

He climbed the stairs, Shandra followed him, and Ryan brought up the rear, using his high beam flashlight to peer into all the nooks and crannies along the way.

At the top, Mr. Shepard unlocked the door and stepped out.

Ryan walked to the edge, sweeping the beam of his flashlight across the top of the building. The metal roof had a slight angle, but nothing treacherous to walk across and fear slipping. He stopped a few feet back from the edge and peered down. The blood-stained paving stones were directly below.

He glanced back toward the roof exit and spotted what appeared to be a smear of something dark colored. "Shandra, shine the light right here."

She eased up to him and held the light while he opened his pack, took out a forensic swab, and rubbed the cotton tip across the smear. He capped the tube, put it back in his pack, and brought out the luminol spray. The smear glowed a nice neon blue. Blood.

"What does that mean?" Shandra asked.

"That you and Mr. Shepard may be right." Ryan put an evidence number next to the smear and took photos down into the courtyard and then back toward the roof exit as well as the number and smear.

"Who has access to the keys for these doors?" Ryan asked as they returned to the multi-purpose room.

"Me and there's a set that hangs in the office." Mr. Shepard closed the door and locked it. "I have a set because I have to go up and check for snow damage in the winter and wash the upper windows there every other month."

The pair of keys that hung in the office could have been taken by anyone. But if the victim had taken them to go up on the roof and jump off, why weren't they on her person after she jumped? "Can you show me where the keys are kept?"

Mr. Shepard strode toward the office. He pulled out a ring of keys and unlocked the office door. Around the corner from the door on a rack next to the teacher's inboxes hung half a dozen keys. They were all labeled. Doors to roof had a key hanging underneath.

Mr. Shepard glanced at him then Shandra. "If Ms. Tait jumped, how come the key is here?"

Ryan nodded. "The same thing I was thinking after not finding a key on her."

"I told you she didn't jump," Shandra said, moving off toward the secretary's desk.

"What are you doing?" Ryan asked.

"The other day, Rachel was doing something on the computer she didn't want me to see." Shandra sat down in the desk chair and tapped the spacebar.

The computer came on.

"We don't have proper paperwork to look at anything on that computer," Ryan said, moving behind her.

Mr. Shepard kept his distance.

"It all looks like items you would find on any secretary's desk," Ryan said, grasping the back of the chair to pull Shandra away.

"This doesn't." She clicked the icon that looked like a viper with rabies. Up popped conversations in a forum.

Chapter Twenty

Shandra couldn't believe the topic of the forum. *Removing scum from our school*. The leader's name was Miss Chevious.

She read down the comments and gasped. "This chat instigated Mr. Huntley's death."

Ryan leaned closer and read. He pulled out his phone and walked out into the multi-purpose room talking as Shandra read on and couldn't believe the way the leader pushed the followers into a heated discussion of the best way to wipe out the scum in their school.

A shudder of revulsion shook her. "This is scary. It reeks of vigilantism."

Mr. Shepard remained standing out of sight of the

screen.

Shandra glanced over at him. His eyes were downcast, and his hands folded in front of him. "Did you know about this?"

"Not that chat, but I knew there was an underground group working on a way to turn the tables on Mr. Huntley. It wasn't just the females who hated him. Their boyfriends and friends saw what his presence did to the girls." Mr. Shepard shook his head. "I don't condone killing the man, but they had played some pretty good pranks on him this year."

She faced the custodian. "Pranks. Who led them or set up the pranks? Was it this Miss Chevious?"

He swiped his nose with the red rag dangling from his pocket and locked gazes. "Don't know anything about a Miss Chevious. Far as I know it was Ms. Tait."

Her breath caught. The woman on her way to forensics.

Ryan returned to the office. "I ordered Rachel be brought in for questioning and a search warrant for this computer." He placed a length of crime scene tape over the monitor and keyboard.

Shandra rolled the chair back from the computer and stood. "Mr. Shepard says Nancy was leading the students in pranks against Mr. Huntley. Do you think she figured out who went too far and killed him?"

Ryan shook his head. "We won't know anything until forensics finishes with her body. Let's go." He grasped her arm, escorting her to the office door. Swinging toward the janitor, he said, "Lock everything up. With this being a weekend, how can we contact you when the search warrant comes through?"

Mr. Shepard grabbed a piece of paper and wrote down a number. "Call me there and I'll let you in."

"Thank you." Ryan led her on out the front of the building and along the sidewalk to where he'd parked his SUV. "I'm taking you home, then going to the station. When they bring Rachel in, I want to know all I can about her."

Shandra nodded. She'd had enough sleuthing for one day. Her heart was heavy thinking about her friend and wondering who had been cruel enough to end her young life.

~*~

Ryan dropped Shandra off and headed straight for the Sheriff's Department. Cathleen said she'd put the reports on Rachel Taylor on his desk. It was close to nine when he entered the building and headed to his office.

"Any word on Rachel Taylor?" he asked Charles Wyland, the other dispatcher.

"Nothing. Can't find her car and her roommate hasn't seen her since she left for work this morning."

"Thank you." Not good. If she had killed Ms. Tait, it sounded like she was on the run. He stopped half way down the hall and backtracked. "Put out a BOLO on her. She may have run."

Charles nodded and started typing.

Ryan shed his coat and hat at the door, dropping them into the visitor chair across from his desk. He opened the top of the file and began reading about Rachel Taylor. He stopped when he noticed her mother's name from her first marriage. He'd read that name somewhere recently. He pulled up his files on this case on the computer and scrolled. Rachel's mother had been one of the first people to file a harassment charge against Huntley seven years ago.

Seven years. Rachel was twenty-one. That would have made her a freshman at Warner High. He wrote down her mother's address in Coeur d'Alene and her phone number. Punching a button on the phone, he called Charles. "Have police in Coeur d'Alene look here." He rattled off the address. "It's her mother's house."

He disconnected and sent requests for Rachel's school records in Coeur d'Alene and her mother's records. There must have been more than the usual harassment for Rachel to have taken things to such an extreme. He read through the rest of her records and noted she had been seeing a psychiatrist before moving to Warner. The therapy hadn't helped judging from what he'd read on the Rid the Scum chat.

~*~

Shandra had trouble falling asleep. Every time she closed her eyes, she saw her friend sprawled on the school courtyard. With Sheba on the bed at her feet, she finally drifted off.

Grandmother stood on top of the school with Shandra. She pointed to all the students with bowed heads standing around the dead teacher. "Are you telling me the pranksters didn't have anything to do with it? What about the group Rachel orchestrated?"

Ella, grandmother, held her arms as if rocking a baby. "There's a baby involved? I don't understand." Ella vanished and so did the students and even Nancy's body disappeared. Shandra stood on the top of the school, alone, and feeling vulnerable.

Pulling on her hair, woke Shandra. Sheba had crawled up the bed and had her paw on the pillow next to Shandra's head.

"Did I wake you with my murmurings?"

Sheba woofed and jumped off the bed.

"Do you need out?" She glanced at the clock. Midnight and Ryan hadn't returned. Had they found Rachel?

~*~

Ryan sat in the interview room with Rachel Taylor. The Coeur d'Alene Police had found her out on the town.

"This will be easier if you just answer the questions." The young woman had done nothing but cross her arms and stare since she'd been put in the room.

"My first question is how did you get Mr. Pawner to hire you as secretary at Warner High School? You had no previous credentials and were only a few years older than the students." He slid the harassment report across the table. "Did it have anything to do with your mother's harassment charges being ignored when she was a teacher at Warner?"

The young woman flicked a glance at the paper then glared at him.

"Did you and your mom cook this scheme up? Get into the school system and start a vigilante group to kill Mr. Huntley?"

When she didn't respond he added. "I guess I'll have the State Police bring your mom in. We'll get her side of this." He picked up the folder and stood.

Finally, the death stare cracked. "No. Don't call her. She doesn't know anything about my job at the school. I told her I'm waitressing."

"Why doesn't she know?" He'd start with the easy, less incriminating questions.

"We loved it here. She was getting over the divorce to my dad and seeing someone. I had made friends and then that scumbag Huntley started cornering her and following her. The guy she was seeing thought she was being paranoid. But I saw Mr. Huntley in the bushes across from our house taking pictures. I yelled at him and he ran off. Then Mr. Pawner said he'd do something about it and he didn't. He didn't tell the school board and he didn't even talk to Mr. Huntley as far as I could tell. And the creep kept cornering my mom. He even did it one day when I was in her room. She'd asked me to wait after school with her, hoping he'd not come in the room. But he did. That was the day, she walked into Mr. Pawner's office and quit."

She leaned forward. "She never got over that. Mr. Pawner was as much to blame as Huntley." Rachel sat back, and her top lip curled in a sneer. "I told Mr. Pawner if he didn't hire me, I'd take my mom's journal, which documented every one of Mr. Huntley's encounters, to the school board."

That was how someone so young was hired. "And did he also agree to your vigilante chat room, Miss Chevious?"

Her body straightened but her face remained pissed at the world.

"We found the chat room and coincidentally, it matches the shredded conversations that were left on my doorstep a day ago along with a smashed clay head." He shoved a photo of the box with the paper and clay across the table in front of her. "Any idea where that came from? I don't think it was you having a conscience."

Rachel studied the photo, keeping her eyes downcast.

"Think we'll find your DNA in the clay? It's at the state forensics lab being tested for anything that would link it to the person who so adeptly reconstructed Mr. Huntley's head. Something only the murderer would know."

She shook her head. "I didn't kill him. I'm glad he's gone, but I didn't kill him."

"Do you know who did?" He pulled out the photo of Ms. Tait in the courtyard. "Did Ms. Tait find out about your little gang? Did you decide she needed to go as well?" He slid the photo across the table.

The woman's intake of breath wasn't faked, she appeared shocked by the photo. "Ms. Tait?" She started to touch the photo and drew her hand back. "How?"

"We're trying to figure that out. It happened about five this evening." He watched as the young woman's eyes flicked to the picture, to the table, and back to the picture. As if she wanted to see it all but was afraid of taking it all in.

"I left for Coeur d'Alene right after school. I bought gas on the outskirts of town. I have the receipt in my purse." She pulled out the words as if putting together an alibi that she thought would work.

"Why did you tell Ms. Higheagle that Ms. Tait wouldn't be in for the rest of the day, when it is evident, she was at the school."

Rachel's gaze snapped up to his. "What are you talking about?"

"I happen to know Ms. Higheagle was anxious to talk to Ms. Tait. She asked you when Ms. Tait would return from her doctor's appointment and you told her she'd called and said she wouldn't be in the rest of the day." He'd opened his notepad as he talked and tapped the information on the page as he'd written it earlier.

"I did say that. But it was only to keep Ms. Higheagle from coming around the office. I was trying to calm down the members of the chat who were spooked by Mr. Huntley's death. I couldn't do that with her trying to peek at my computer all the time."

"So, Ms. Tait had planned to be at the school in the afternoon?"

She shrugged. "As far as I knew."

Ryan stood. He wasn't sure what to do with the woman. But he'd keep her locked up until they'd had a chance to read all of the online chats. "We'll be holding you until I get the search warrant for your computer at work and we can go through the conversations you had with the students."

"You can't do that. Can you?" For the first time since she entered the room, Rachel looked like a scared young woman.

"I can keep you on suspicion of murder." He opened the door. "Delong, will you put Miss. Taylor in one of the holding cells, please."

The young woman deputy, nodded, and entered the room, escorting the shaken Rachel to the cells.

Ryan went to his office and replayed the conversation. Was hauling this woman in a dead end? He didn't think she'd killed Ms. Tait. But did she instigate the murder of Huntley and had one of the students decided Ms. Tait knew too much and killed again?

Chapter Twenty-one

Shandra sat in Ryan's kitchen staring out at the beautiful blue sky and wishing she were home, on Huckleberry Mountain. But with all that had happened, there was no way Ryan could get away and she felt obligated to stick around so he had someone to run ideas by.

It was nearly nine. She didn't want to work on her pottery but was at a loss for what to do.

Ryan rarely slept in, even when he'd been out till early morning, but this morning, she had let him sleep and it appeared he'd needed it. Sheba woofed at the back door. Shandra padded across the kitchen to the door and let her in.

Shandra hadn't awakened enough when Ryan came to

bed to tell him about her dream. This morning, it had played over and over in her head, making her wish she could chase it away. But until she told Ryan about it, she wanted to keep all the details fresh in her mind.

To keep from dwelling on it, she began making pancakes.

"Good morning," Ryan said, entering the kitchen.

"Good afternoon, sleepyhead." She handed him a cup of coffee.

"I deserve that. I can't believe I slept this long." He sat down at the kitchen table and scrubbed a hand over his face.

"Did they find Rachel?" She continued making the pancake batter.

"Yes. She blackmailed Pawner into giving her the job."

Shandra stopped scooping flour and studied him. "Blackmailed?"

"Her mother was the first person to file a complaint about Huntley and the first one to be ignored." Ryan sipped his coffee.

"Is that why Rachel started that online group?"

"It appears so." He walked over to the cupboard and pulled out two plates.

The batter hissed as she poured it onto the griddle. "Did she admit to Nancy's death or why she lied to me?"

Ryan placed the plates and silverware on the table and stood by her. "She was in Coeur d'Alene by the time Ms. Tait was thrown off the roof. She lied to you because she didn't want you coming around snooping at her computer." He put a hand on her shoulder. "Your snooping may have broken the case open, once we get our hands on the chatting that went on in Miss Chevious's chat room."

She hoped that some good would come of her wanting to find the truth. "Did she say if she knew who actually killed Mr. Huntley?"

"No. And she's too smart to point a finger at anyone she might have been chatting with. It would make her an accomplice."

Shandra put four cooked pancakes on a plate and handed it to Ryan. "I had a dream last night."

"Finish cooking those and come join me," Ryan said, taking the plate to the table and grabbing the butter and syrup.

She poured four more pancakes onto the griddle. When they were cooked, she balanced them on the spatula and added the four to the pile on the plate. She sat down and told Ryan about her dream. "The more I think about it, I don't think it was someone from Rachel or Nancy's followers who killed Mr. Huntley. And I would bet that Nancy figured it out and that's why she was killed."

"Ms. Tait was ruled out as a suicide once the forensics team put together all the evidence. She was killed by a blow to the back of the head before she was thrown off the roof."

Shandra shuddered. Did Nancy even suspect what was coming? A blow to the back of the head, the blow to Mr. Huntley was taken from behind him. The person had enough rage to kill but enough humanity to not be able to look their victim in the face as they did it.

"None of it makes sense. What are you doing today?" Shandra asked, poking her pancake with her fork.

"I'm going to try and piece together Ms. Tait's movements yesterday and call on the teachers she may have had contact with."

Shandra stopped her fork midway to her mouth. "And

Mr. Pawner. Mr. Shepard said he saw him and Nancy arguing."

"He's at the top of my list." Ryan finished off his breakfast and put the dishes in the sink. "What are you going to do?"

"I'm going grocery shopping and then coming back and doing laundry." She wrinkled her nose. "Not my favorite things, but I'm not feeling creative at the moment."

Ryan stood beside her chair. He pulled her up into his arms. "I'm sorry we couldn't go to your place this weekend. As soon as this is solved, and you are done volunteering, we'll hide out at the mountain for a while."

"I'm going to hold you to that promise."

He kissed her and headed into the living room. She heard him put on his coat and pick up his backpack. The door closed, and she placed her plate of pancakes on the floor for Sheba. She already had plans to do an around-about trip to the store.

~*~

Ryan had left orders at the station to have a deputy pick up Mr. Pawner for questioning this morning. When he arrived at the Sheriff's Office, he found Mr. Pawner sitting in the lobby waiting.

"Thank you for coming in." Ryan stuck out his hand to shake.

The principal stared at his hand a moment before shaking hands. "It didn't sound like I had a choice."

"You always have a choice but coming in and answering questions could help us discover who killed two of your teachers." Ryan motioned for the man to follow him.

They walked down the hall to the interview room. He motioned for Mr. Pawner to enter. After the man was settled in a chair, Ryan said, "I'll be right back. Would you like some coffee?"

The man nodded.

Ryan left the door open, to let the man know he wasn't being held against his will. He dropped his coat and pack off in his office, grabbed the files on the two cases, and two cups of coffee out of the break room.

He walked back into the room and found Mr. Pawner texting. "Do you take it black or need cream and sugar?"

The man's head snapped up. He focused on the cups and said, "Sugar, please."

Ryan retraced his steps to the break room and brought back several packets of sugar.

Pawner opened two packets and drizzled the white crystals into his cup.

"The reason I asked you to come in is because I learned last night that you and Ms. Tait were arguing before she was thrown off the roof."

The man's gaze flashed from his cup to Ryan. "Thrown off? What do you mean? I thought she'd committed suicide."

"The forensic lab says she was dead before she hit the ground. There wasn't any hemorrhagic bruising where her body landed across a pile of snow, only abrasions. And she had been hit on the back of the head but landed on her face. There was also blood on the roof that didn't match her blood type and was typed as a male. Someone else was up there." He studied the man.

Pawner was chewing on his bottom lip. "We now have two murders at the school." He shook his head. "I can't believe it. Do you think it was the same person who killed both of them?"

Ryan couldn't tell if the man was curious and worried

or if he was trying to change the conversation from his confrontation with Ms. Tait.

"I think Ms. Tait figured out who killed Mr. Huntley." He stared at the man. "I think she was telling you when Mr. Shepard saw you two talking."

The principal shook his head. "She wasn't telling me about who killed Huntley. She said she knew that Rachel was running some kind of chat room that praised bullying and put ideas into student's heads." He held up his hands. "I told her, I'd look into it, but she was adamant I should do something right then. I have to appear before the school board on Monday to tell them about Mr. Huntley, how I looked the other way, and I don't have time to deal with something like an online chat."

"Even if that could be what caused both the murders?"

Pawner's gaze met his. "You think Rachel's rantings could have caused the death of Mr. Huntley?"

"There were a lot of women and young girls hurt by his actions. From what I've gathered even their brothers, boyfriends, and fathers were up in arms over how you looked the other way. I'm surprised they didn't string you up as well." Ryan didn't usually let his own personal bias come into the interview room, but having two sisters, he understood how vulnerable a teenage girl could be. And that the man had preyed on the teachers…And nothing was done to stop it. The man sitting in front of him could have done something but had let money sway him to ignore the complaints.

Pawner had the decency to nod. "Looking back, I would have done things differently. But it's too late now."

"So, for the record, you say Ms. Tait wanted you to do something about Rachel's online chat group? That's what you were arguing about?"

"Yes."

"Do you know where she went after she talked with you?" Ryan had been recording the whole conversation, he was also making notes.

"I assumed to her office."

"You weren't worried she was going to get into it with Rachel?" He studied the man across the table from him.

Pawner picked the cuticle on his left thumb. "I told her not to. That I would handle it. She wasn't happy, but I figured she'd wait for me to do something."

"Even knowing how little you did for the victims of

Huntley's harassment?"

The man flinched. "I was still her boss."

"Do you know if anyone else saw her that afternoon?"

"You could look in her appointment book or ask Kathy, she had the office next door to Nancy." Pawner picked up the coffee and downed it all in one long drink.

"Thank you for coming in." Ryan stood and waited for the man to leave.

Once Pawner was gone, he opened the file and found Kathy Jones address. He planned to see her next and ask her if she'd seen Ms. Tait the day before.

Chapter Twenty-two

Shandra parked her Jeep in front of the Lawrence house. The car that had followed her the other night sat in the driveway alongside the same pickup.

She stepped out of her vehicle as the front door opened.

Mrs. Lawrence had a purse and keys in her hands. She glanced out toward the street and frowned. "What are you doing here?" she asked, not taking a step off her porch.

"I'd like to talk to Lenny." Shandra strode across the lawn and up to the woman.

"Why?"

"Did you know that Ms. Tait was murdered yesterday?"

"We heard something on the news. The kids are

moping around. I was going to go to the store and get ingredients for sundaes." The woman's fiery demeanor sputtered today under the mourning of another teacher.

"Would you mind if I talk to Lenny and Lana while you go to the store?" Shandra was going to talk to Lenny one way or the other. The boy was always popping up around the school and seeing things.

"I don't like it, but I also don't like how many teachers are showing up dead. I want answers as much as my kids and the other parents." She nodded and opened the door.

The two teenagers sat on the couch staring at music videos on the television.

"Ms. Higheagle wants to visit with you while I go to the store." Mrs. Lawrence nodded to a chair and left, closing the door behind her.

Lana gave her a weak smile. "Did you hear about Ms. Tait?"

"I did. That's why I wanted to come visit with you. See how you're doing." Shandra sat in the chair and shifted to face the couch and the two quiet students.

"I'm okay. Still can't believe Ms. Tait, a counselor, would take her own life." Lana shook her head as she stared down at her knees. Her fingers played with the frayed edge of the hole in her pants.

"She didn't take her life. Someone else did."

Lenny's gaze shot to her. The tips of his ears turned red.

Lana gasped. "Another one?"

"We, Detective Greer and I, believe that Ms. Tait had figured out who killed Mr. Huntley." She didn't wait for any reaction just trudged on. "And we know about the Rid the Scum online chat group and Ms. Tait's pranks on Mr. Huntley. My biggest fear is that a student is behind all the deaths." She studied the brother and sister. "I really don't want to find out that either of you had a part in it."

Lana leaned forward but Lenny squirmed.

"I helped Ms. Tait with some of the pranks on Mr. Huntley, but I didn't know about the online chat other than overhearing a couple of people talking about it." Lana faced her brother. "You should tell her what you know."

"Lenny, both Detective Greer and I know that you followed me the night I visited the Langes. Did you take the clay head from my Jeep, and then put it and the shredded online chat on his porch?" Shandra reached out a hand. "I don't believe you had anything to do with the murders, but I do believe you might know more than you've told us so far."

"Lenny, do you? You are always wandering around the school and talking to everyone." Lana poked her brother's arm. "You're going to make a great investigative reporter someday."

"Lenny, what do you know?" Shandra tried to appear supportive while wishing she could squeeze the information out of the young man.

"I knew about the online chat. After being part of it, purely to know what was going on, I realized what Miss Chevious was trying to do. She wanted someone to take out Mr. Huntley, AKA, The Scum." He shrugged, raising his hands. He had a band aid on a finger. "The conversations didn't sound like anyone was taking her serious but then when he was killed, I started rereading what all had been said. There was one person who seemed overly eager to make The Scum pay. That's when I shredded the online chat to give to the police."

"Did you make the clay head that I found in Travis's cubby hole?" Shandra asked.

"No. I don't know where it came from, but I saw you take it out and put it in the box. I figured it had to mean something that's why I followed you to see where you were going. While you were in Boyd and Travis's house, I logged onto the chat and someone in there was saying how they were sure that Travis, the retard, had killed Mr. Huntley."

Shandra shook her head. "That chat had become vicious." If she could get her hands on Rachel right now, she'd give her a lecture on common decency.

"When your dog came running at me, I left but circled around because I didn't see you take the box into the house. I wanted to make sure Detective Greer found out about the online chat, but I didn't want anyone to know I did it. I have a reputation as someone you can tell anything, and it won't leak. That's how I keep my eyes and ears on everything."

"Including all the women and girls Mr. Huntley harassed?" Shandra glanced over at his sister.

Lana wore a frown.

"When I discovered Principal Pawner wasn't doing anything about it, I figured nothing could be done." Lenny gave his sister an apologetic wince.

"The day Mr. Huntley died, did you see or hear anything unusual?"

"Mr. Huntley chewed on Mr. Shepard, but that seemed to be a daily thing. I think because Mr. Shepard broke up a lot of Mr. Huntley's harassing the girls. Ms. Miller told Huntley off after Travis ran out of the Art Quad. You saw Boyd put Huntley up against the wall. That was epic!"

Shandra agreed in her head but on the outside, she raised an eyebrow.

"Well, you know, someone finally standing up to the old pervert." Lenny's eyes gleamed.

"After lunch, before Ms. Miller found the body, did you see anything?" Shandra willed the young man to think of something.

"No. I was in charge of showing the class how to do a process on the computer. That's when Ms. Miller left."

"How long was she gone?" Shandra didn't think petite Gertrude could have swung anything hard enough to have caused the damage but one never knew.

"She left about twenty minutes into class and never came back. We all found the back door locked when we went to leave after class and that's when we learned about Mr. Huntley." He shook his head. "Ms. Miller wouldn't hurt him. She can barely move some of the equipment in the room around."

"So somewhere between the time class started and twenty minutes later, Mr. Huntley was killed." Shandra tapped her finger against her chin. That wasn't a very long time frame to get a prop from the prop room, confront and kill the victim, and return the prop all without being seen.

"What about yesterday afternoon. Did you see Ms. Tait?" Shandra decided to move on.

"I did. I was finishing my lunch when she walked in. I went over to ask her something and she walked right by me as if she didn't see me." Lana's bottom lip came out in a pout.

"I was told she had a doctor's appointment in the morning and wouldn't be in in the afternoon." Shandra waited to see if either made a comment.

Lenny jumped in. "She didn't have a doctor's appointment."

"How do you know that?" Shandra asked.

"Because I heard her tell Ms. Miller she was going to

get to the bottom of all the outlandish behavior at the school."

"When did you hear this?" Shandra had to give the young man credit. He definitely had his ear to the pavement when it came to the school.

"The afternoon before. I heard her tell Mrs. Jones that she wouldn't be in tomorrow morning, she had an appointment to take care of the problems at school." Lenny shrugged. "I figured she was going to the school board. That's what mom does when she's unhappy with what's happening at the school."

Shandra studied Lenny. Had Nancy gone to the school board? Mr. Pawner had already sent in his resignation, or so he said. He would be the only person other than the killer who would be threatened by a visit to the school board. Especially considering how he hired Rachel.

The door opened, and Mrs. Lawrence walked in carrying a grocery bag. "I have all the sprinkles, nuts, and toppings you two like." Her gaze landed on Shandra.

"I'll let you enjoy the rest of your Saturday." She stood and faced the twins. "Thank you for talking with me. I hope we get this all cleared up soon. I want you to feel safe at school." Shandra motioned for Mrs. Lawrence to follow her.

At the door, she asked, "Who on the school board do you think a teacher would go talk to?"

Mrs. Lawrence studied her a moment then said, "Mr. Tulley and Mrs. Simon. They are the two who get things done."

"Thank you." Shandra exited the house and glanced at her phone. It was nearing noon. She texted Ryan. *Do you have time for lunch?*

Within seconds came the reply, *Meet you at the deli.*

She climbed into her Jeep and headed to the east side of town. The deli was two blocks from the Sheriff's Department.

~*~

Ryan sat in a cozy kitchen in the home of Mr. and Mrs. Jones. Kathy was the other counselor at Warner High and had the office next door to Ms. Tait.

"I'm sorry to bother you on a Saturday and after such emotional news," Ryan said, picking up the coffee cup the woman had placed in front of him when she invited him into the kitchen.

"I still can't believe someone killed Nancy. I found it hard to believe she'd commit suicide, as the news first reported but someone killing her…" Mrs. Jones shook her head as tears glistened in her eyes.

"Did you speak with Ms. Tait yesterday?"

"Only briefly. She'd said her meeting in the morning had been successful." Mrs. Jones sipped her coffee.

"Meeting in the morning? I thought she had a doctor's appointment?" Ryan was feeling lost.

"No, that's what she told nosey Rachel. She had a meeting with someone on the school board. She was going to put an end to all the shenanigans going on at the school." Mrs. Jones nudged a plate of cookies toward Ryan.

He ignored the treats and focused on the woman. "Do you know what shenanigans and who she talked to?"

"I don't know who she talked to, but she and I had been told about this online chat where kids talked of doing things to the teachers they didn't like, and she thought it might have had something to do with Mr. Huntley's death." Mrs. Jones covered her mouth with a hand. "My word. Do you think that's why someone killed her?"

Ryan was having the same thoughts. He needed to

discover who Ms. Tait talked with from the school board and hope forensics had come up with an image on the surveillance tapes.

Chapter Twenty-three

Shandra walked into the deli and spotted Ryan right away. He sat at a table in the corner near the front of the store. Two sandwiches, pickles, chips, and two waters sat on the table.

She sat down and picked up a water. "Thank you for ordering."

"I wasn't sure when you'd get here, and I can only take thirty minutes, ten of which are gone." He picked up the sandwich closest to him and unwrapped the white paper. "You were doing more than getting groceries this morning."

She studied him. He already knew where she'd been. "Yes. I spent some time with Lenny and Lana."

"Without their mother present." He raised an eyebrow.

"She was headed to the store when I arrived, and I asked if I could talk with them. I was as shocked as you when she said yes and left. But I did learn, it was Lenny who put the shredded paper and clay head on your porch." She went on to tell him everything she'd learned.

"Mrs. Jones said that Ms. Tait had an appointment with someone on the school board yesterday." Ryan picked up a pickle. "I wish I knew which one."

"Either Mr. Tulley or Mrs. Simon. That's who Mrs. Lawrence said would get things done."

Ryan pulled out his phone and dialed.

"Charles, could you text me the addresses for a Mr. Tulley and Mrs. Simon. They are school board members. Thanks." Ryan studied her. "I suppose you want to go along while I ask questions?"

"Well, I did come up with the names…" She bit into her sandwich to hide the grin tickling her lips.

They finished their sandwiches and walked to her Jeep.

"Why don't you take your Jeep to my house. I'll come by and pick you up in about thirty minutes. I need to go to the station and add my latest interviews to the file." Ryan leaned on her open Jeep door.

"Okay, Sheba will like a chance to go outside for a while." She kissed his cheek and closed the door. She hoped they could discover what Nancy had learned that ended her life.

~*~

Ryan returned to the station where his SUV was parked and headed straight back to his office. Opening the screen on his computer he spotted a new email from Sheila Rickman at the Forensics Lab.

He opened the email and read: The blood sample is B positive, not the victim's type and is from a male. Hypothesis: the killer fell while carrying the body to the roof and scraped a limb, leaving the smear in the photograph. If there hasn't been any increment weather, trace evidence could be hooked on the object that caused the injury.

Ryan pulled out his notepad and dialed Mr. Shepard's number. As he waited for the man to answer, he opened another email. He had his search warrant for the computer at the school.

"Hello," Mr. Shepard answered.

"This is Detective Greer. I have the search warrant and

I need to do some more evidence gathering, can you meet me at the school in ten minutes?"

"I can be there." The phone went dead.

Ryan printed out the search warrant and had Deputy Trapp called to meet him at the school.

On the way to the school he called Shandra.

"Hello," she answered.

"I'm going to be a bit later than planned. The search warrant came in for the computer. I'm headed to meet Mr. Shepard and Deputy Trapp at the school. I'll swing by and get you when I finish there."

"I'll be here."

He hit the end button and hoped she didn't decide to find the school board members on her own. It did take less time having her talk to people while he did other tasks like gather evidence, but she put herself in danger and put his job in danger by using a civilian for a lot of his information.

Mr. Shepard stood inside the main doors when he arrived. Deputy Trapp pulled up as Ryan opened the door. The deputy caught up to him as he held the door and waited.

Ryan moved to the office. Mr. Shepard unlocked the door and picked up an empty copy paper box sitting beside a desk.

Deputy Trapp and the custodian loaded the computer into the box and Ryan wrote out a receipt for the computer and keyboard.

"Take that out to your vehicle and come back. We need to look for trace evidence on the roof." Ryan waited inside the multi-purpose room as the custodian held the doors for the deputy. The two walked over to where he stood by the door leading to the roof stairs.

"What are you looking for?" Mr. Shepard asked.

"I'm not sure. Once you unlock the door at the top you need to remain down here."

The custodian nodded. He unlocked the doors and left.

Ryan stood at the roof door. "Over there about ten feet is a blood smear. Forensics said it isn't the victim's. That means the killer scraped on something getting up here or while carrying the body on the roof. Look for something jagged and fibers in the stairwell. I'll look around up here."

Trapp pulled out a flashlight, nodded, and started a slow descent of the stairs.

Ryan studied the door and door jamb looking for anything that might snag or scrape. Nothing. There was a cupola with a spinning vent. He moved to the vent and checked it for corners or loose pieces.

"Greer!" Deputy Trapp called from the stairwell.

Ryan worked his way to the door and stared down. "Did you find something?"

The deputy shone his light on a rough edge of the fourth step from the bottom.

Removing his backpack, Ryan knelt on the same step. He pulled out his camera and the luminol. After taking several photos from different directions, he sprayed the area.

The glow wasn't as bright as the smear on the roof, but who knew how many times they'd stepped on the spot going up and down the stairs. He swabbed the blood with an evidence collector, used tweezers to pick at everything along the rough edge and put it in a small plastic bag. When he believed he had gathered everything that might pertain to the crime, he labeled it all and put it in his pack.

"Makes you wonder if it was a small person trying to pack the victim up the stairs," Deputy Trapp said.

Ryan could see someone catching their foot on the woman's skirt as they started to climb the stairs and land a shin on the edge of the step. "I'd think a small person would have dragged the body up the stairs." He flicked on his flash light and searched all the steps for any sign of blood or fabric. He found skin and blood on two more steps.

When he was sure they wouldn't find any more evidence, he nodded to the door at the bottom of the stairs.

Mr. Shepard stood by the door leading out into the courtyard. He seemed lost in thought.

"You can lock up now," Ryan said, handing the evidence they'd collected to Trapp. "Take these and the computer to the forensics lab. Rickman will be waiting for them."

Trapp nodded and left the building. His siren screamed to life and died away as the deputy headed toward Coeur d'Alene.

"What did you find up there?" Mr. Shepard asked.

"Evidence that might point us to the killer." Ryan walked toward the main entrance. "Did you notice anyone limping when they left yesterday?"

"Boyd Lange, but I figured it was from basketball. Don't remember Mr. Pawner limping but he'd changed. He was wearing sweats. He said he'd ran laps while the team practiced."

"Did he run laps often?" Ryan knew Shandra would be angry if he didn't try to find someone other than the obvious, Boyd Lange.

"Every so often he ran in the gym after school. Usually when he had a meeting in the evening." The custodian closed the doors and locked them.

Ryan stood on the front steps of the school. He'd pick up Shandra and speak to the school board members, then he'd go by himself to the Lange house.

Shandra heard Ryan pull up. She called Sheba in from the backyard and had her coat in her hands when Ryan entered the house.

He grinned. "I'm surprised you didn't run out and jump in as I slowly rolled by."

"Funny." She wasn't sure how to tell him she knew which school board member they needed to talk with. "I made a couple calls while you were busy."

Ryan's forehead furrowed into a scowl. "Who did you call?"

"Mr. Tulley and Mrs. Simon. Nancy talked to Mrs. Simon, but she told me to call when we were headed her way and she'd have Mr. Tulley come over to be included." She picked up her phone. "Shall I call her now?"

"Who did you say you were when you called?" Ryan walked by her and into the kitchen.

Water ran, and he returned with a full glass. As he sipped, his gaze locked with hers.

"I told her who I was and why we wanted to talk with her. She was agreeable. She said she didn't for a moment believe that Ms. Tait would kill herself. She was a woman on a mission." Shandra walked over to the door.

Ryan emptied his glass, placed it on the end table, and motioned with his hand. "Call her."

Shandra made the call, and they headed to the woman's home on the west side of town.

"What does this woman do for a living?" Ryan asked as they pulled into a circular driveway with a nearly four thousand square foot house behind it.

"Her husband is in construction. She has a real estate

office." Shandra had looked the woman up while waiting for Ryan.

They exited the SUV and walked up to the front door. Shandra rang the doorbell. They waited only thirty seconds before the door opened.

"Ms. Higheagle, Detective, come in." The woman led them into a dining room set with cookies, a coffee urn, and tea pot. She turned to them and held out her hand. "I'm Margery Simon."

"Detective Greer," Ryan said, shaking hands.

"Shandra Higheagle," Shandra said, shaking the woman's hand and immediately liking their hostess.

"Please have a seat and help yourself to the cookies. Daniel should be here any moment. He just lives down the road. I called him after Ms. Higheagle called and gave him a head's up." Mrs. Simon sat across the table from them. "This business at the high school is awful. Two teachers in less than a week. It's not safe for teachers or students. We had a board meeting last night. Several of the members thought we should shut the school down until the person responsible is caught." She peered at Ryan. "Do you have any idea who did this?"

"I'm following leads and the state forensic lab is working around the clock on all the evidence we've sent them."

Shandra could tell Ryan was holding back, but she also understood holding back information helped them to catch the guilty party.

The doorbell rang.

"That will be Daniel. I'll be right back." The woman strode from the room.

Shandra faced Ryan. "How much do you want me to say?"

"Just follow my lead. If I look at you, add in what you know." He picked up a cookie and nibbled.

Mrs. Simon entered with a man a decade older than herself. He was tall, thin, and sported a bushy white mustache.

The woman made the introductions and seated the newcomer next to her across from Shandra.

"I'm not sure why you wanted to speak with Margery," Mr. Tulley said.

"Ms. Tait had a meeting with Mrs. Simon yesterday morning. We believe whatever was talked about may have been the catalyst for her murder." Ryan leaned forward.

"Coffee or tea?" Mrs. Simon asked, pouring a cup of coffee for Mr. Tulley.

"Coffee," Ryan said.

"Tea," Shandra offered and picked up a cookie. Either the woman was being evasive, or she was that perfect of a hostess.

Once everyone had a beverage the woman said, "She was telling me about all the harassment allegations against Mr. Huntley and how Mr. Pawner hadn't lifted a finger to do anything to stop it. I asked her to bring me the reports and I'd make sure that it was looked into. She also said she believed that Mr. Pawner was behind an online forum that had worked up the students to cause harm to Mr. Huntley."

Ryan glanced at Shandra. She wasn't sure if he wanted her to speak or if he was figuring out what to say.

She decided to jump in. "I-we've talked to all the women who filed the reports and some of the students who—"

"Students?" Mr. Tulley interrupted. "You mean this teacher, Huntley, was also sexually harassing the students?"

Shandra couldn't believe this was the first the man had heard of it. "Yes. Didn't you get Mr. Pawner's resignation?"

The two school board members looked at one another.

"No, this is the first we've heard of the resignation," Mrs. Simon said.

"Mr. Pawner told me the day of Huntley's death when we'd discovered the harassment reports, that he was turning in his resignation." Ryan pulled out his notepad. "Who would that have gone through?"

"The superintendent and then it would have been brought to our attention." Mr. Tulley said, pointing at Ryan's notebook. "And if George didn't notify us after receiving it, especially given this new light, he'd better be writing his own resignation." The older man pulled out a cell phone and stood. "I'm going to call him right now."

Mrs. Simon nodded and offered the plate of cookies. "We'll get to the bottom of this. I didn't realize this had been something that no one had addressed."

"Were you aware that Mr. Huntley was the grandson of the Dalworths?" Shandra asked, already certain the woman wouldn't have let the family's money make a difference in how she handled the situation.

"The Dalworths are great benefactors to the high school, but I didn't know that the deceased was their grandson. I'll have to send my condolences." The woman pulled out her cell phone and typed.

"Mr. Huntley preyed on the female teachers and students at the high school. He not only made them uncomfortable at school, he followed them in the evenings, taking photos of them." Ryan's words caused Shandra to shudder, thinking about how the man had stalked each of the females he'd made a victim.

Mrs. Simon stared at Ryan. She scowled. "Do the Dalworths know this about their grandson?"

"I had the impression the grandfather did, but the grandmother doted on him." Ryan poised his pen over his notepad. "Did you and Ms. Tait talk about anything else other than that you wanted the files?"

"No. I told her to bring me the files and I'd make sure something happened, though I didn't know what since the person they all blamed was dead." The woman's mouth dropped open a second before she snapped it closed, then asked, "Do you think one of the teachers or students he harassed had had enough?"

"There were more than his victims involved. There were fathers, brothers, and boyfriends." Ryan cast a glance at Shandra.

What did he know that he hadn't told her?

"That many people knew what was going on and the school board didn't get a hint of it? My goodness, how long?"

"Seven years" Ryan said as Mr. Tulley entered the room.

"Seven years?" Mrs. Simon's face darkened with rage. "Mr. Tulley, did you know that there was a teacher sexually harassing teachers and students at the high school for seven years?"

"I just found out about it. Mr. Pawner did turn in his resignation. George was trying to find a way around him losing his tenure and retirement before he handed it to us." Mr. Tulley shook his head.

"The man doesn't deserve that if he let so many teachers and students be harassed for that long." Mrs. Simon's voice rose in indignation.

"I agree, but we'll be fighting George and anyone else

who believes we need the Dalworth's money." Mr. Tulley said the Dalworth name as if it left a bad taste in his mouth.

Shandra studied the two. "Now that this has come to light, will there be some changes made at the high school?"

Mrs. Simon nodded. "There will be. I'll also make sure there is restitution. The Dalworth's can afford to pay the families and pay for counseling at the high school."

Shandra smiled. She understood why Mrs. Lawrence said these were the two to deal with school issues.

"Thank you for the refreshments and the information." Ryan stood.

"You'll let us know as soon as you find out who killed Ms. Tait?" Mrs. Simon asked.

"Yes. I'll make sure you receive the statement." Ryan grasped Shandra's elbow, leading her out of the dining room.

Shandra thought it telling that the woman didn't care who killed Mr. Huntley. If not for justice, no one would care, except his grandmother.

Chapter Twenty-four

Ryan dropped Shandra off at his house and promised he'd bring home something for dinner. He didn't want to tell her he was headed to find out why Boyd Lange was limping when he left school on Friday.

He parked in front of the Lange house. All the lights were on, giving him the impression the family was home. Ryan walked up to the door and rang the doorbell.

A heavy step resounded on the other side and the door opened.

Mr. Lange stood in the doorway. "Detective."

"I have a couple of questions for Boyd. I'm sorry if I'm intruding on your dinner…"

"We hadn't sat down to eat yet. Come in." Mr. Lange moved out of the way, and Ryan walked into the entryway.

"This way," Mr. Lange said, waving a hand toward the living room.

Ryan entered. The two brothers were playing a game on the television.

"Boyd, the detective would like to ask you a question," Mr. Lange said, motioning the young man to get up and come to them.

Boyd, cast a glance their way and slowly put the game controller down. He stood up, winced, and limped over to them.

"How'd you hurt your leg?" Ryan asked.

"Came down wrong on it in practice and sprained it." Boyd lifted his jogging pant leg and revealed a bandaged ankle.

"Dr. Sprat says if he stays off of it, he'll be able to play in next week's game," Mr. Lange added.

"Could you lift your pant leg a little higher. I'd like to see your shin?" Ryan believed the two, but he wanted to make sure he'd checked thoroughly.

Boyd glared at him but raised his pant leg. No scrapes or scratches.

"Thank you. Did you happen to see Ms. Tait on Friday

afternoon?" He decided to ask not expecting anything of value.

"Yeah, she and the secretary were going at it." Boyd let his pant leg drop.

"What do you mean 'going at it'."

"Arguing. The secretary gave Ms. Tait a shove." The young man glanced over at the television where his brother played.

"Where and when was this?" Ryan pulled out his notepad.

"Last period. They were over in the corner of the multi-purpose room. I was going to the office for Mr. Timms when I saw them."

"Did you see them on the way both to the office and back?"

"Just on the way there. The secretary must have seen me, because she came hurrying over. I don't know where Ms. Tait went." Boyd glanced at the television again.

"Thank you, Boyd." Ryan let the young man get back to his game. He tapped his notepad. He needed to get back to the department and question Rachel Taylor before her twenty-four hours were up. If he didn't find more evidence against her, he'd have to let her go.

"Thank you for allowing me to talk to Boyd," Ryan said, shaking hands with Mr. Lange.

"We have nothing to hide. What were you looking for when you asked him to raise his pant leg?"

"I can't tell you. It's part of the investigation. Good night." Ryan walked out the door and over to his vehicle. Inside the SUV, he texted Shandra. *Dinner will be late. I have to talk with Rachel Taylor one more time.*

I'll get something. She texted back.

He wasn't sure if he was relieved she was going to take care of it or worried that she would go talk to someone she shouldn't. *OK,* he replied.

When he entered the sheriff's office, his phone buzzed. "Greer."

"This is Lou at the forensic lab. I've been able to pick up the imaging that was deleted. I'm sending it to your email. And we sent you all the transcripts from the Rid the Scum forum. It's interesting reading."

Ryan had no doubt it would be. "Thank you." He hung up and glanced at the time. Six-thirty. He had until one A.M. to talk to Rachel. He'd rather read through the transcripts and have seen the image from the surveillance cameras before he talked with her.

He should stay here and go through it all, but he wanted Shandra to look it over, too. Make sure he read it the same as she did. He did an about-face and headed back to his vehicle.

~*~

Shandra did a quick search of Ryan's refrigerator and cupboards before making a list and heading to the grocery store. It was hard to cook at his house because he had so little. His schedule kept him away from home during most meals.

She pulled into the grocery store and stepped out of her Jeep. Sheba sat in the back seat, her nose sticking out the six-inch opening Shandra had left in the window.

"Be good," Shandra said, and headed into the store. She had a list of items and grabbed a shopping cart.

She raised up from plucking a package of noodles off the shelf and spotted Mr. Pawner walking down the aisle pushing a cart. A woman walked on one side of him and a teenaged girl on the other.

"Ms. Higheagle, what a surprise," he said, without any

warmth in his voice.

"Mr. Pawner. It appears we both are shopping for dinner." She smiled at the two women.

"Margo and Lucy, this is the famous potter who has been volunteering at the school." The principal started pushing the cart as if to move on by.

"It was a pleasure meeting you," Shandra said, noting the items in their shopping cart. Ice cream, pizza, bandages, and antiseptic cream.

She continued gathering her items and stood in line to check out. The Pawner family walked out of the grocery store together, but the women went to a fancy car and Mr. Pawner climbed into an older pickup.

He didn't call them his wife and daughter, though that is what they appeared to be. She tucked that information away for later. Before getting into her Jeep, she received a text message from Ryan saying he was home.

She hurried back to his house and found him staring at an image on his computer.

"I'll have shrimp fettucine ready in fifteen minutes, if you can make the salad." She packed the two grocery bags into the kitchen.

He grunted and followed her.

"What were you looking at?" she asked, unloading the bags and setting the salad ingredients by the sink.

"The surveillance footage. I think it's a male. He definitely knew about the cameras. The person is wearing a hoodie and they held the prop between them and the camera while carrying it out and back in." Ryan unwrapped the lettuce and washed it.

Shandra started water boiling and gathered her ingredients for the fettucine sauce.

"Could you tell if they were tall, short, anything on the hoodie that might help?" She worked on the main course as Ryan tore the lettuce and cut up other vegetables to go in the salad.

"Comparing him to the door frames, the person is closer to six foot than five foot. Which could be half of the males at the school. My nephew Bobby fits that description." Ryan tossed the salad and placed the bowl on the table. He wandered to the cupboards and pulled out dishes.

"But you're sure it's a male?" Shandra still wasn't convinced that Rachel didn't have something to do with both murders.

"Yeah, it's clear enough to see a male build. The hoodie isn't loose…" He left the room and came back with his laptop. "In fact, the hoodie is a bit small."

Shandra poured the cooked noodles into a strainer and stepped over to take a look at the computer screen. "I'm surprised it hides the person's face so well considering how it rides up on his arms and waist." She stared at the photo. "He's wearing sweatpants."

Ryan stared at her. "How can you tell that?"

"Look at the way they poof at the ankles. They have elastic. That makes them a sweat pant or athletic pant whichever you want to call it." She returned her attention to the grilling shrimp and fettucine sauce.

When it was all ready, she tossed the noodles in olive oil, then the sauce, and topped it with the grilled shrimp. "Here you go."

She placed the plates on the table and filled a glass with wine before sitting down.

Ryan closed the computer and grabbed a cup of coffee before joining her.

She raised an eyebrow. "Coffee. Does this mean

you're going back to the station after we eat?"

"After we eat and we both read the transcripts from the chat forum." He twirled noodles onto his fork.

"You have the transcripts too?" This was going to be an interesting evening.

"Yes. I want you to read them and see if we both understand what Ms. Taylor was trying to do." He held up a speared shrimp. "This is really good."

"Thank you. It's the quickest thing I know to make." They continued eating and making small talk.

"I ran into Mr. Pawner at the grocery store. He introduced me to his wife and daughter. I think?" She still wasn't sure about the dynamics of the three.

"Wife and daughter? From what I've uncovered he's separated from his wife." Ryan studied her. "You're sure it was a wife and daughter?"

"He only introduced them by their names. Margo and Lucy. But I had the feeling they were a family until the women got in a fancy car and he got in an old pickup." She still wondered over that. "I know families do meet in separate vehicles to do things together, but the vehicles were so…different. I don't know."

Ryan pulled out his phone and started texting.

"What are you doing?" Shandra raised her wine glass.

"I'm having dispatch run everything they can find on Russ Pawner." Ryan finished texting, and they finished their dinner, saying little.

Shandra cleaned up the kitchen while Ryan made two copies of the transcripts. When she entered the living room with a cup of tea for her and coffee for Ryan, he was already reading the chat forum.

She sat down on the couch and began reading. Within ten minutes, her anger started to boil. "What is wrong with Rachel? She is getting half a dozen students worked into a vigilante frenzy."

Ryan looked over at Shandra. He knew she'd be more emotional reading the transcripts. He'd read many things like this and worse in his law enforcement career. "You can stop reading."

"No. I want to help. Did you notice, she barely conceals who The Scum is. Any student who walks through the Art Quad would know who she means. He was the only male teaching in the quad and she makes fun of his unbuttoned shirt and 70's porn-star mustache. These kids weren't even born then, and neither was she. How did they know what she was talking about?" Shandra set the papers down and took several sips of her tea to let her mind grasp the depravity that Rachel had shown her followers and then asked them to do her bidding. There were two, who appeared to hang on her every word and were eager to help her initiate justice.

Ryan pulled out his phone and dialed. "Lou, this is Detective Greer. That transcript I had you download. Can you find out who The Joker and Shade are in real life?"

Shandra found the two names. After reading their replies to Miss Chevious, she understood why he wanted to know who they were. "Did you see what Shade said about Nancy? I wouldn't doubt that person had something to do with her murder." Reading the malicious comments the followers of the group suggested as ways to get back at teachers, made her wonder that more "accidents" hadn't happened around the school.

"I think I have enough to go have another chat with Ms. Taylor." Ryan stacked his transcript papers and pulled a file out of his backpack.

A photo slipped to the floor. Shandra picked it up. It

was the back of a naked young woman. "Why is this in the folder?"

"That's one of the photos I found at Huntley's place." Ryan studied Shandra. "Why? Do you know this person?"

"I'm not sure, but it could have been Lucy. The girl I thought was Mr. Pawner's daughter."

Chapter Twenty-five

Ryan returned to the sheriff's department and requested Ms. Taylor be brought to the interview room. As he walked by dispatch, Wyland handed him a file. He carried it and his backpack into his office.

Opening the file, he discovered that Russell Pawner and his wife Margo had filed for a separation. They did have a daughter named Lucy. He looked at the photo of the family from a school event and had to agree with Shandra that Lucy looked a lot like the naked young woman in the photo from Huntley's apartment. Had the man started following around the principal's daughter?

His phone buzzed with a text.

Shandra.

I forgot to tell you that there were bandages and

ointment in the Pawner's shopping cart.

Things were starting to stack up in favor of the principal.

Ryan grabbed his files on the two murders and entered the interview room. Ms. Taylor didn't look as stubborn as the first time he'd chatted with her.

"Do you know who Shade and The Joker are on your chat?" He decided to start with that and work his way to the fact she'd been seen arguing with Ms. Tait before the teacher's death.

"No. And no one knows who Miss Chevious is. I set it up that way, so everyone could say what they wanted without anyone knowing."

"You didn't want anyone to find out you were instigating a murder."

"No! I didn't plan for him to get killed. I wanted him caught and fired." She crossed her arms.

"That's not what your comments sound like. You asked your followers to make The Scum's life miserable because the world would be better off without him in it. Those are words to make a follower think, Mr. Huntley should be killed." Ryan pulled out the transcripts. As he'd read, he'd used highlighters to mark Miss Chevious, The Joker, and Shade's comments. "If you read the comments by these three, it sounds like a murder is being planned. Right down to using the stage props."

She shook her head. "I didn't plan his murder."

"What about Ms. Tait's? I have a witness who saw you arguing with her near the stairs to the roof."

Her face paled. "A witness?"

"Yes. I'd like you to pull up your pant legs."

She frowned. "Why?"

"Whoever carried Ms. Tait's body up the stairs fell and left their skin on a step and blood on the roof." He stood and walked around the table. "Lift up your pant legs, please."

Ryan waited as the young woman slowly folded her pant legs up to her knees. There weren't any scratches or recent scrapes on her legs. But one had a large scab. "What happened there?"

"My friend and I were motorcycle racing."

"You do know that if we discover either Shade or The Joker killed Mr. Huntley and Ms. Tait, you will be an accessory because of the forum and how you urged them to rid the school of scum."

She put her hands on her face and started to cry.

Ryan picked up his folders and left the room. He asked the deputy standing outside the door to release Ms. Taylor.

She might be an accessory, but he didn't think she'd killed anyone. He dropped the files into his backpack, shut down his computer, and headed home. He couldn't think of anything else he could do tonight.

Shandra sat on the couch reading the transcript after Ryan left. The conversation ran all the way up until the forensic techs printed it out. Miss Chevious had obviously tried to talk down The Joker and after Mr. Huntley's death Shade had stopped commenting. Had Shade been Lenny? He'd said he'd been on the forum to monitor what was going on. Lenny wore sweatshirts. She didn't like the way her thoughts were going.

After a cup of chamomile tea, she drifted off to sleep on the couch.

The transcript scrolled in the background as the young woman, Lucy, stared into a mirror. Was this all connected to the photo Mr. Huntley took of her? Ella sat on a cloud not moving or saying a thing. If the deaths were caused by the photo of this girl…Mr. Pawner was the murderer. She shuddered thinking how many lives the man had hurt. Could he have been so calloused to go all the way to murder?

A door closing and a soft woof, yanked her from the dream and to a groggy consciousness.

"Sorry, didn't mean to wake you," Ryan said, placing his backpack on the coffee table and shucking out of his coat.

"I needed to wake up. My dream was only confusing me more." She sat up and made room for him on the couch. "Did you learn anything that will help solve your cases?" She picked up her tea cup and sipped the cold brew.

"I don't think Rachel Taylor had anything to do with the actual murders, but her forum might have instigated them. Making her an accessory." Ryan wandered out of the living room and returned with a beer.

"You must be done for the night," she said, nodding toward his beer.

"I am. The woman and girl you saw Mr. Pawner with are his wife and daughter. Though they have a legal separation." He pulled the file out of his pack. "It appears the daughter goes to a Christian high school."

"With what Mr. Huntley was doing, Mr. Pawner probably wanted to keep his daughter away from the pervert."

"Yeah, but the photo I found at Huntley's looks a lot like Lucy Pawner. I'm thinking Huntley went too far by following her." Ryan's phone buzzed. He pulled it of his belt.

"Greer." He listened.

"Thank you." He hung up the call and said, "Damn!"

"Who was that?" Shandra rose to get a refill of tea.

"The forensic lab. The blood and fibers we found on the stairs up to the roof are that of the victim, Ms. Tait."

Shandra stopped. "That means she was dragged up the stairs, not carried. Mr. Pawner would have been able to carry her." Her thoughts shot back to Rachel.

"According to Boyd, Rachel was arguing with Ms. Tait and pushed her." Ryan sipped his beer.

"Do you think she killed Nancy, dragged her up the stairs, and tossed her off the roof?" Shandra wandered into the kitchen and started the tea kettle. She returned to the living room. "Did she have an alibi for the time of death?"

"Yes and no. If Ms. Tait was killed after their argument, Rachel does have an alibi. She purchased gas on her way out of town and the time stamp on the receipt is four-thirty. Mr. Shepard saw Ms. Tait fall about five." Ryan patted the couch next to him.

Shandra held up her finger and returned to the kitchen to replenish the tea in her cup. She returned and sat by Ryan. "But Boyd saw Rachel arguing with Nancy last period. So around three. That's two hours before she was thrown off the roof."

"And thirty minutes after Rachel got gas." Ryan pulled out his note pad and started a timeline.

"You know, Rachel could have easily fueled her car and returned by five and tossed Nancy off the roof."

"That would mean she killed her before she set up the fake suicide." Ryan tapped his notepad. "And it doesn't account for the fresh blood smear on the roof. It was from a male."

"She was working with someone. You said before that someone had to have Mr. Huntley's attention when the killer hit him with the prop." She stared into her tea. "Do you think that maybe the murder was a prank gone wrong? They had planned to just knock him into the wall and he ended up hitting his head and dying?"

"Whose prank? The Rid the Scum group or Ms. Tait's pranksters?" Ryan circled Rachel and Nancy's names on his notepad.

"Do you still have Rachel in custody?" she asked.

"No. I let her go. I didn't have enough to keep her any longer. Why?"

"If she was in on the two murders, do you think she'd get in contact with the other person who helped her?"

Ryan sat up. "That's a possibility." He pulled out his phone and dialed.

"Sheriff Oldham, I'd like to put surveillance on Rachel Taylor." He listened.

"Yes. I have reason to believe she had an accomplice in the murders at the high school and I'd like to see who she contacts."

"Yes, I understand. Thank you." Ryan closed the connection then dialed again.

"This is Detective Greer. I'd like your patrol cars to locate a car."

Shandra listened as he rattled off the make, model, year, and license plate of Rachel's car.

"Yes, when it's found I'd like to be contacted. No, I don't care what time it is. Thank you."

He pulled the blanket on the couch over them. "That's settled. Let's see if we can get some sleep while we wait for the call. Once they locate her, we'll start following her."

Chapter Twenty-six

Rachel and someone with red hair were running down a path. Shandra called out to stop, but they only ran farther. She could feel their fear and when they grabbed hands and jumped off a cliff, her heart lodged in her throat, but she managed u scream.

"No!"

"Shandra, wake up. It was just my phone. They've located Rachel's car." Ryan's voice broke through her dream.

She shook her head and pushed awake. "It's Rachel and Lenny."

Ryan already had his coat on. "You better stay here."

"No. I need to go. They might do something stupid. In my dream they jumped off a cliff." Shandra shot to her feet and grabbed at her coat, her quick motions made her unsteady on her feet.

"Hey, slow down. Her car is at her apartment. She's probably in bed asleep." He helped her put her coat on. "It's after midnight."

She shoved her arms in, grabbed her purse, and headed for the door.

They drove Ryan's SUV across town and sat a block down from Rachel's apartment and waited.

"Can't you tap into her phone or check her records?" Shandra asked.

"I have requested a subpoena to get her phone records, but that won't come through until later today if they can get a judge to sign off on it on Sunday. Or Monday. If your dream is correct, she and Lenny are going to make a run for it."

As if he were conjured up from their thoughts, the car that had followed Shandra when she visited the Langes, slowly rolled down the street. It barely stopped and someone opened the door, tossed in a bag, and jumped in. The car sped off as the door slammed shut.

"There's our answer." Ryan started his vehicle and fell

in behind at a leisurely pace, keeping them in sight.

"Are you going to pull them over?" she asked.

"They haven't done anything wrong that we know positively. We have no proof either one of them killed Huntley or Tait." Ryan picked up the car radio. "I have suspects in sight. Do not apprehend. I want to see where they are going. Over."

"Can I call Mrs. Lawrence and ask for Lenny's phone number?" Shandra wanted to connect with the two. Help them see it was better to turn themselves in than run.

"If you call and wake her up and she realizes her son is gone, she may tell him we're looking for him. Right now, he doesn't have a clue we're following. Best to keep it that way."

Shandra wasn't sure she agreed, but he had more experience with this than she did.

The car continued out of town, heading north on Highway 95.

"Do you think they are going to Coeur d'Alene?" she asked.

"Could be. That's were Rachel's mom lives. Once they get out of the county, I'll have to call in the State Police."

Ryan pushed the transmit button. "Dispatch this is Detective Greer. I'm following suspects north on highway ninety-five. Request state police back-up. Over."

"Will give them notice. Dispatch over."

When Ryan finished talking, the car ahead of them put on their blinker and turned right.

"They're headed to Shoshone Park," Shandra said, having read the signs along the highway.

Ryan reached for the radio and pressed the button. "Dispatch, this is Detective Greer. Send State backup to Shoshone Park. Suspects just headed that direction. Over."

"Affirmative, Dispatch over."

"I hope they aren't going to do anything stupid." Shandra said, holding onto the arm rest with one hand and the dash with her other as she leaned forward to keep the tail lights in sight.

"Don't think the worst. They could just be finding a secluded place to discuss what to do next."

Shandra stared out the front window. "Or one of them is getting rid of the other to clean things up."

Ryan shifted his attention from the road to the woman in his passenger seat. "Why do you think that?"

"Neither one has given any indication of being the killer, yet one of them has to be. And if that person has killed twice, what's to keep them from killing again to hopefully stay out of jail?"

He didn't like her line of thinking, but it was quite possible, Lenny brought Rachel out here to kill her. It made sense since it was his car and he'd picked her up. No one would know where she went. And everyone would believe she was the killer if she came up missing.

The car stopped in the deserted parking lot by a picnic area.

Ryan turned off his lights, rolled the Tahoe to a stop and shut off the engine.

"Now what do we do?"

"Let's see what they do and where they go." His phone buzzed. It was Sargent Peel of the State Police.

"Sgt. Peel. Are you backing me up?" Ryan asked, keeping his gaze on the two young people piling wood in a fire pit.

"I am. Just turned down the road to Shoshone Park."

"Turn off any siren or lights. I'm watching the suspects. At the moment, they're making a fire. You can pull up behind me and we'll advance on foot." Ryan closed the connection and watched as the two pulled packs out of the car.

"Do you think those are clothes with blood on them?" Shandra asked. Her hand moved to the door handle.

"Stay. Sgt. Peel will be here in a minute. I'm going to keep them from tossing those on the fire." Ryan exited the vehicle not even shutting the door to avoid the two hearing anything.

The gravel road crunched under his shoes. Ryan made his way to the side of the road, keeping his eyes on the two suspects. At their car, he crouched down and listened.

"Once we burn these clothes, they can't get us for anything," Rachel said.

"We should have told them it was an accident. A prank," Lenny said.

"Do you think they'd believe us? That cop is trying hard to pin both the murders on me. I'm not going to jail for two accidents. And you're the one who hit Huntley." Rachel opened her pack and pulled out a sweatshirt. She walked over to the fire and held it over the flames. "Come on. Throw your sweatshirt in here."

Ryan stood up. "Police! Put your hands in the air!"

Lenny dropped the bag and raised his hands.

Rachel dropped the sweatshirt in the fire and took off at a run with the pack.

"I have him," Peel said, running up behind Ryan.

Ryan took off after the young woman. "Rachel, stop!"

She continued running right toward the river.

"Rachel, stop!" Shandra shouted.

He didn't know how she'd reached the river before he did, but she stood between the woman and the water.

Rachel stopped, her raspy breathing was easy to hear over the muted sounds of the river.

"You don't want to make this worse," Shandra said, walking towards the young woman.

"I don't want to go to prison," Rachel said, and flung her bag at Shandra.

Shandra deflected the bag. "If you didn't kill anyone, you won't. You did all of this as revenge for your mom. Don't make her childless. Stand up for what you did."

"It was all a prank. A way to humiliate him like he did all the girls." Rachel's voice had the whine of a small child.

"A prank. Then it was an accident." Shandra moved

closer to the young woman as Ryan also advanced from behind. "Who hit him?"

"Lenny. I was keeping him distracted and Lenny hit him with the prop. It was just supposed to put glitter all over him and make him muddy if he fell on the ground. He wasn't supposed to hit his head. He wasn't supposed to die."

Ryan grabbed Rachel's arm and pulled it behind her back. He had her cuffed by the time Shandra had her arms around the young woman.

"What about Nancy Tait?" Shandra asked.

"Another accident. She came to me all angry, saying she knew about my forum, she knew I'd instigated Mr. Huntley's death. She said she was going to tell the police. I told her she wasn't any better. That I knew about her pranks and crusade to torment him as well. She called me a name. Words like that shouldn't come out of a teacher's mouth. I got angry and shoved her. She hit her head on a table and I didn't know what to do. I propped her up around the corner where hopefully no one could see her. When I helped Boyd with Mr. Timm's roster, I grabbed the key to the stairs and pulled her in."

Ryan led her back to his vehicle. Shandra carried the bag.

"How did she get on the roof?" Shandra asked.

"I called Lenny and told him what had happened. I told him if he didn't do something with her body, I'd tell the cops he'd killed Mr. Huntley and it was all his idea. He was Shade. He was the one who came up with the prop idea and offered to get it. He said, he'd take care of Ms. Tait. He'd drop her off the roof to make it look like suicide."

Ryan shook his head. If the two hadn't covered it up, they could have received a lesser sentence for accidental homicide, but covering it up… He wasn't sure what they would get.

Chapter Twenty-seven

Shandra felt bad for Mrs. Lawrence and Lana. Neither one had any clue Lenny had been caught up in the two murders.

The students and faculty were so distraught the school board closed school for a week. Shandra wasn't sure that was the right thing to do. They needed to see one another and know that life would go on and that their school would come out of this a better place to be.

Mr. Pawner was removed immediately, and the vice principal took over until the board found a suitable replacement. Shandra took the week the school was closed down to return to her place. She'd missed Huckleberry Mountain, her studio, animals, and even Lil.

"You going back to that school when it reopens?" Lil asked as they saddled horses to go for a ride.

"Yes, I have two more weeks left. I don't want to let the students down." Shandra hoped she'd see Lana Lawrence. The girl had been beside herself the last time they'd talked, after her brother had been arrested.

"How long will you be here before you go off to your aunt's?" Lil walked Sunshine, her horse out of the barn and into the spring sunlight.

"I should be here a month to six weeks. Just enough time to get another vase made. Why?" Shandra mounted her horse, Apple.

Sheba stood at the start of the path up the mountain, her tail wagging and her tongue hanging out in anticipation of a good walk.

"Just wondering. It seems like you've been gone more than you've been home lately." Lil headed up the trail.

"I feel the same way." She breathed in the scent of pine and the crisp spring air and wondered why she ever left this heaven.

About the Author

Thank you for reading *Artful Murder*. This storyline came from headlines and a bit from my past. As most stories do, they have a bit of the author's life and a heavy dose of fiction. Keep reading the series to be part of Shandra and Ryan's wedding and to see what other murders they help solve.

If you enjoyed this book, please leave a review. It is the best way to thank an author for an enjoyable read. I love to hear from fans. You can find all my social media sites and contact information through my website.
http://www.patyjager.net

All my work has Western or Native American elements in them along with hints of humor and engaging characters. My husband and I raise alfalfa hay in rural eastern Oregon. Riding horses and battling rattlesnakes, I not only write the western lifestyle, I live it.

Shandra Higheagle Mystery Books
Double Duplicity
Tarnished Remains
Deadly Aim
Murderous Secrets
Killer Descent
Reservation Revenge
Yuletide Slaying
Fatal Fall
Haunting Corpse

 Windtree Press

Thank you for purchasing this Windtree Press publication.
For other books of the heart, please visit our website
at www.windtreepress.com.

For questions or more information contact us
at info@windtreepress.com.

Windtree Press
www.windtreepress.com

Hillsboro, OR 97124